Found

Julia Biagi

Copyright © 2015 Julia Biagi

All rights reserved.

First Edition, 2015

ISBN-13: 978-1508896210

Cover Design: Qiane Hale

This novel is a work of complete fiction. All characters and events portrayed in this novel are either products of the author's imagination or are used fictitiously. Any similarities to actual persons are coincidental. Unfortunately, some of the circumstances are common, but these characters and events are created from the author's imagination with no intention to portray any non-fiction/actual persons, living or deceased, or to portray any past, present, or future situations related to non-fiction/actual events.

To David:

*Thank you for believing in me
and for empowering me to
chase my dreams.*

ACKNOWLEDGMENTS

Thank you to all of you who made this novel possible through editing, prayer, coffee dates, pep talks, and countless other ways. It took a village to carry me through every step of this process,
so thank you (in no particular order):
David Biagi, James and Jayne Osburn,
Adam and Jayme Pervis, Jim and Pat Lamb,
Robin Tennille, Chris and Anna Harper,
Tim and Charissa England, Angela Reuter,
Kasey Couch, Susan Ryan, Sara Robb,
Chris and Brooks Reid, Johnny Satterfield,
Adam and Catherine Hiltner, Christina Sheer,
Clyde Lewis, Duan Davis, Leslie Walker,
Mark and Rosanne Bowen, and Qiane Hale.

To my countless other friends, family, teachers, and professors, there isn't enough space to name all of you without writing a whole new book, but trust me when I write that your encouragement, teaching, and love carried me through when I needed it.

"All I want is to be safe,
to be taken care of,
and to be loved.
I'm pretty sure I have at least one of those things,
but I'm not sure which,
or if I can even have all of them at the same time."

-Jenny, age 12

[Untitled]

Three parts

Abandon

Unspoken

Found

Three voices

One with no sound

One trying to find a voice

One sharp, distinct voice

Three notes, one chord:

C major for guitar

C

E

G

Who pulls the voice-strings

-Jenny, age 12, winning poetry contest poem

DUSK AT THE ESTATE
Anni

I stood by a window staring at a maple tree on the front lawn. My vision blurred and shifted with evening haze as I imagined Seymour chopping wood, despite the heat: His walnut face blistering red with every swing of his axe; his undershirt sleeve rolled up out of his long abandoned smoking habit; the short whistle as each split came to completion.

    Even during the summer, he demanded a fire on Saturdays. His daughter once told me of a time when she was small before they installed an air-conditioning unit on her parents' farm. She said that it was an insatiable summer where even the birds seemed too close to stewed for singing or flying. Regardless of swimming through humidity and heat, Seymour demanded his Saturday fire that weekend. The sun had not even touched the horizon as he lit the kindling and forced the entire family to sit before the fire with the windows open and not a breeze passing through to squelch the heat. Only when his daughter passed out did Seymour release them from the room, but he remained in his chair with sweat rolling from the top of his head to his toes. He always got what he wanted even if it made him sweat for hours while his wife, son, and housekeeper revived his daughter. She laughed as she told the story, but I never knew if she laughed out of embarrassment or bitterness.

There I stood by the window, staring at the maple, and imagined Seymour swinging the axe somewhere through the haze. I knew with some certainty that the axe swung at least two counties away, but my tired eyes could see him right down to the faded Wranglers and shiny brown work boots. As the imagined yet real axe fell and split a log, tears leaped onto my face. I could almost hear the axe crash into the log, shredding through the dried fabric and fibers of pine. When I should have heard his whistle, I realized my pot of tea water was singing in the kitchen.

I blinked slowly at the maple tree before the vision of Seymour beside it faded into the mosquitoes and gnats and a lone lightning bug. I moved toward the kitchen with the stupor of one caught in a dream. For a second, I thought I heard the familiar voice of a girl. Was that a cry? I felt my feet break to a run toward the back of the house through the kitchen. Was she here? Had he--? I threw open the kitchen and screen doors. At break-neck speed, I caught my shirt on a chair-back, which spun me around into a trip. A hole snagged into the shirt; my hands kissed the stone porch; and my knee bent into a scrape on the ground. A horse whinnied from behind the stables. I shook myself awake from the stupor. The neigh mixed with the teapot whistle.

The teapot!

The teapot sputtered and cried in a single angry note from its cobalt throat. I limped inside while fumbling with the rip in my shirt. I found myself apologizing to the teapot as I transferred it with bruised, dirty hands from the burning eye. Why could I apologize so easily to a teapot? The tea whistle settled. I grabbed my oversized, polka dot mug that looked more like a soup bowl. The teapot water continued to bubble as I poured it over jasmine green tea. I placed a tile over the mouth of the cup.

While the tea steeped, I gently cleaned my hands and scraped knee. I checked the Dali kitchen clock's exploding face for the time before placing the tile on the counter. I delicately made my way back to the front room and settled in my chair with my foot propped up to watch the pitch black thunderheads roll in from the west. My eyes and thoughts drifted away from the window. They traveled up, up, up with the tea water steam to the ceiling and into the bedroom where the morning's fight darkened my entire day...

A fight between lovers is only more difficult when it is a fight between married lovers whose very being vibrates within the other at every moment of every hour of every day. Sometimes we forget that we aren't the same person. Sometimes we remember that we are different. Other times I remember that he isn't Christopher. That reminder usually happens suddenly and leaves me awash in grief. This Saturday was different. This Saturday, at the pinnacle of our argument, I reminded him that he wasn't Christopher.

The words shot off my lips like little arrows poised and aimed for his perfectly shaped heart. He stepped back once...then twice. My hands rose slightly, but they didn't fly to my lips to push the words back into my throat. His jaw set. His hands rose with palms flat toward me by his ears. My words stopped hovering in the tension and sank deep into his chest.

"No. I'm not Christopher," he agreed so quietly I almost didn't hear him.

I started to say something. It came out in a puff of nothingness that followed his figure backing gently out the door. His eyes left my face and followed his feet. I felt his vibration pull from deep in my core and move with him out of the house. I remained standing in the middle of the room while staring at the empty doorframe. My heart pounded in my ears, but I was still trembling with the reason for the venom of "You aren't Christopher!" My mouth opened and shut over and over with the efficiency of a fish.

I lingered in that spot for an eternity. I barely noticed the sound of his footsteps going down the stairs and heading out the door. My blood in my ears hid the sound of his car leaving the estate grounds.

His absence shaded my day. I busied myself with housekeeping so that I could procrastinate having a true reaction to the fight. Despite all my efforts, the alone-ness of my day caught up with me when I finally sought rest. I held my cup of tea with the remnants of daylight disappearing under a shield of a summer storm. My table lamp cast the only glow in the house and reminded me of another house where my absence surely wasn't missed.

I realized I was beginning the slippery slope of wallowing into things I couldn't change and people I had no permission to set free. I took a deep breath wanting to pray, to reach out to God, but my heart fought my mind. I sipped my tea without tasting it and chewed on the past instead of resting in the moment.

The front door opened with a stick and a trip as Peter finally arrived back home. I jumped to catch him despite being twenty feet away from him. Our eyes met. His smile appeared barely more than a frown in the foyer's darkness. He towered like a wet grizzly making a puddle in the foyer.

"Mrs. MacKensie would kill me if she knew I let you drip a lake on her 'daddy's walnut floors,' " I smiled, trying to be normal.

"Ugh that woman," he groaned. "Even after death she chastises you."

"Welcome to the South, where women's memories are long, and their mothering never, ever ceases."

"Don't I know it?" his smile increased as I unbuttoned and pushed his coat off his shoulders.

He shook his hair off to splatter me. I jumped back and laughed. His coat fell to the floor behind him. He kissed my nose and pulled me close. For a moment, it was yesterday when he arrived home from work at the restaurant. He smelled like wet fire, garlic, onion, and hickory. His deep brown eyes were weary and beginning to wrinkle from years of smiles.

"Did you go to work?" I asked as he began to dip for a kiss.

"Yeah, so?" he continued his bend to my much lower in stature lips.

I broke the embrace with a step away from him. His brows furrowed. The emptiness of the day came rushing back to me, and I felt a cry knotting in my throat. I had wondered and pushed out of my mind where he might have escaped to all day. The realization stung fresh that he went to the place where he wasn't Christopher and no one who knew Christopher would be there. I pressed my hands together and sort of began to bow out of the room. The bruises on my hands reminded me of the back porch and the girl's voice that was the horse's whinny. Each new angle of pain pressed my core away from him.

With tears blurring my vision, I missed his scruffy face change from softly puckered lips to furrowed brows and a set jaw. His large calloused hands began to reach for me. The tidal wave of my baggage swept between us. I blindly missed those hands and arms reaching out to me. No matter of blinking could erase the geyser attempting to spew out of my heart from my eyes. I turned away from him with hunched shoulders and simply crumbled to the floor on my already scraped knees. The pent-up cry from this morning finally, desperately erupted from my throat.

His arms encircled me and crushed my nose into his shoulder. All thought emptied my body as I curled into his lap on the floor and wept. He murmured soothing sounds into my scalp. Time stopped as the storm raged around the house.

After soaking his chest and my own face with snot and tears, I started to speak and so did he. We smiled and looked down at our laps. I leaned into him, and he rested his chin on my head. We remained poised and breathing in unison while our hearts mended back together in the silence.

"I'm sorry," he whispered

"For what? I overreacted. I'm the one taking everything personally lately and--" he cut me off while maneuvering me to face him.

He took a deep breath and said, "Moving away from that little girl that you absolutely adore was the most difficult decision you had to make at the tail end of a couple of years of mourning Christopher's passing. Then, we got married, and I moved in here to the house he left you. Things haven't exactly been simple for us, for you. Honestly, you've been ready to burst for a couple months now."

Amazingly, my body still had enough liquid left to form more tears that silently trickled down my face as I nodded and looked at my bruised hands. He lifted my chin to look at him despite the ugly grimace that crying twisted my face into every time. As if reading my mind, he laughed, "You're beautiful." I groaned and pushed him because I was content to believe he was lying for my benefit.

"Do you really think I've been ready to burst?" I chortled.

"Um...haven't your dreams about her been getting more frequent? And you keep talking about that family, and it's been at least a year and a half now since you left. You haven't moved on from them, and--" he stopped himself.

I leapt at his pause to finish his perceived thought, "And you think I haven't moved on from Christopher, but I am. You married this ball of widowed wacko anyway. You knew--"

He shook his head. His square jaw was set firm.

"What? If not, then--"

"You have to stop beating yourself up over what happened. You keep blaming yourself."

I would have stood if the wave of memories hadn't collapsed onto my chest with the force of an angry gorilla: the light in my hand; her little pale face; the crook of Seymour's arm behind his head; the blank stares from the grandmother and mother; the days that followed in silence and denial; the guesthouse where I lived and how the walls seemed to be caving in on me...The memories piled and piled. I blinked and gasped for air. My eyes saw a little girl with a jar wanting me to catch fireflies with her on the back lawn. The vision hovered for a moment as she laughed and reached for my hand. I blinked and she disappeared like her voice that was the horse whinny.

"Who else can I blame, Peter?" I argued after the milliseconds (lifetime) that passed with the memories stacking on my chest. "I stood there, and I tried to get her help, and they just acted like nothing was wrong. They looked at me like I was asking for a cup of sugar!"

"You did everything you could! You have to let it go. You tried everything, but without proof and everyone in denial, you have nothing. That sweet little girl is too afraid to say anything. You have nothing. You tried. You gave it everything you had, but in the end, you had to leave. You had to move out of that sick place!" his voice rose with emphasis, but he was almost pleading with me to believe him.

Oh God, I wanted to believe him. With every fiber of my being, I searched his face and felt his body's warmth. I got on my knees and hugged him. Tears were streaming down his face. My whole consciousness was poised ready to believe him, but that awful voice was screaming in my head with shame and blame and utter failure.

"We both wanted to save them Anni," he whispered.

He had never said that to me. For months, he endured long conversations during our courtship where I lamented and raged and worried over what to do and what I had seen. The denial in that house was so thick that there were moments I had to replay it in my mind to remind myself it really happened. I told Peter in an effort to remember that I lived in reality, not on that stage they masqueraded as a home. When I finally moved out, he refused to let me collapse into bed for a few weeks to wallow in defeat. He even married me despite the incessant talking and worrying and fussing over my choice to move. In all that time, he perfected the art of being an amazing man, but not once did he say that he wanted to help any of them.

"You did?" I asked, pulling back slightly to see his face.

"Of course, I did," he scrunched his brows and frowned. "Nobody wants that for a house full of women. They deserved better than what Seymour did to them."

"Is doing to them," I corrected automatically.

An epiphany light shined from within his face after I spoke. In the year after I moved out and then the six months since we had been married, not once did Peter realize that what haunted me most was the present tense of their situation. His hands cupped my face and pulled me forward so that our foreheads touched.

"So that's why you keep saving that room? You're saving it for her, aren't you?" he said with eyes closed.

"Mmhmm," I mumbled, afraid to speak--afraid to admit it with words.

"I'm sorry. I didn't understand—"

I moved my hands to cover his that cupped my face. His eyes opened. He stopped speaking because I had stopped crying. He held my gaze.

"How could you? You aren't in my head. I'm sorry I never told you that part of me hopes she escapes and comes to live with us," I sighed, "but I guess this means it's time to let go…of a lot of things."

Grieving is a tricky thing. Just when you think you have moved on…that life has moved to a new season that you can handle…it rushes back in a wave of unexpected memories and emotions. Grieving my first husband's death is something people understand and respect, even with marrying Peter, but the grief of saying good-bye to that little girl felt for so long like a grief of no closure but an open wound to my spleen.

As Peter and I rested in the foyer under our conversation and the evening storm, I could almost hear the Lord's voice gently breaking through to my heart. My being flooded with peace, and for the first time in 18 months, I realized that the wound had actually healed and that I had let the baggage go instead of worrying or attempting to fix it.

"You okay?" he asked softly while helping me stand up.

"Better," I smiled unconvincingly.

He hugged me and pulled me to the stairs. He was still dripping from running through the storm from the car to the house. Reluctantly I followed him, but I hesitated at the top of the stairs. Peter kissed me on the cheek as I lingered there as if he already knew what I was about to do. His footsteps faded the opposite direction into the master suite. I stared down the door where the memory of our morning fight faded into the sage colored walls. The very sight of the door pulled me toward it, and suddenly I was standing in the middle of the room as though transported.

I had not seen nor spoken to the child in eighteen months, but somehow, that room continued to be my little sanctuary of hope. When the grounds or house were used for photography shoots or weddings, I used that room for the extra equipment or a coatroom. I had debated making it another bridal suite for weddings, but I couldn't bring myself to choosing a chaise or even paintings to place in the room. My heart longed for that little voice to chirp in my ear, "Oh Anni, let's get that one!" I slowly turned in the center of the room. For the first time, I allowed myself to imagine it full: white-painted four-poster bed with clean lines and a plum quilt, silver frames with photographs of butterflies and roses, a white table for a desk covered in stacks of notebooks and homework, a color-block carpet in cool tones, and clothes everywhere. Her head peeked out of the closet with a huge grin, and as she started to speak, I reached out to touch her cherub face. Thunder clapped and starkly burst the phantasm. Lightning flashed a moment later to illuminate again the barren walnut floor and empty walls. I noticed the curtain rod that Peter hung early that morning to surprise me. Lying over two chairs stolen from the dining room were the most elegant white curtains. They were satin that looked like full-fat milk cream. I picked up one of the panels and felt a gasp loose through my lips. I ran my palms ever so lightly over the fabric, memorizing the rough yet gentle touch of the fibers. Peter had been about to hang curtains when I entered the room that morning. Instead of dwelling on the fight, I moved the chair to the window and began to hang the curtain panel. The fabric swished like a bride walking down the aisle.

 My mind drifted away to a world that I had forgotten in a photography studio in Paris. Lerner had taken a job for a bridal couture spread for Vogue. I was in the middle of adjusting lights as he threw a tantrum over the models lack of poise. The words sounded measured, almost out of a script. I remember laughing to myself and wondering for the millionth time why he took this job.

 "Apprentice!" he raged, causing me to jump in surprise. "Bridal couture is sheer lunacy when I could be eating at Diane's this very moment!"

 I started to remind him that Diane and Jacques only served a very exclusive dinner service, but he thrust the camera in my hands.

"It is your time Annice!" he yelled.

And like that, the apprentice took her place as lead photographer for a six-page spread in Vogue that the editor saw fit to extend to ten. I took my favorite shot standing on a rickety chair that Lerner himself held steady while Nicole lay on a bed of peacock feathers and navy silk. She turned so perfectly with her dress puddling as gently and immobile as if carved from marble. Lerner had grumbled something about her surprising ample bosom causing shadow issues, and I responded in a mocking voice about my own bosom, which caused Nicole to sputter in laughter. You can't fake the color that shown in her cheeks and throat from the hearty laugh we shared. I snapped at least eight pictures in those few seconds, and the last still held color in her marble face and neck with a laugh stifled into a smirk and knowing in her eyes. Lerner christened the photograph *Anni's Mona Lisa Bride*. Later, he took Nicole and I to an intimate dinner on 10th in Paris to surprise us with an advanced copy of the Vogue with Nicole on the cover. I still don't know how he got his hands on it the night before release, but to this day, I have my copy in the studio behind the house.

I really should call him when he gets back from Hong Kong, again, I thought to myself. I stepped off the chair and looked at the curtain my husband naively bought to help me begin to fill this room.

"It reminded me of Mona Lisa's dress," he said in the doorway while flipping on the light.

I jumped two feet in the air and stumbled into the newly emptied chair. I attempted to not knock the chair over which caused me to fall on the floor.

Peter dove toward me laughing, "I'm sorry I startled you; I'm so sorry..."

"What is it with chairs today?" I grumbled, my bruised hands stinging anew.

"What do you mean?" he asked while righting the chair and stood me on my feet as though I was light as a feather.

I shook my head and waved his question off. He didn't press it. Instead, he planted a kiss on my forehead before placing me in the chair.

"How about I finish this job for you?" he offered while practically tossing the curtain on the rod in a fraction of the time it took me.

I walked over and adjusted the panels over the window. "Now all I need is a--"

Peter held a wide silver scarf for each panel. "I thought you might like these as tie-backs. I already put some straight post hold-backs on the wall, but I thought this would soften the room for another bridal...er...whatever you wanted this room for."

I took the scarves with my mouth open. I think I made a sound or a gush. He laughed. The scarves were from a boutique I dragged him to once because a high school friend was opening it with her sister. I remember telling Peter that Clara would never steer a person wrong to make a sale.

"I love you, but there is no way you came up with that on your own," I looked up at him with glassy eyes.

"Clara said that I came to the right place, and I quote, 'Curtains are the eye shadow for a room. Sometimes you need some sparkle to set them apart.' Then she found these that you've apparently been pining over?" he smiled with mischief and pride. (Oh why had we not had this conversation that morning)?

With shaking hands, I tied the curtains back with the scarves. The silence shook with silk and satin. I rejoined Peter's side a few paces from the window. He looked at me to evaluate my impression. I could feel his eyes on me, but I concentrated with an almost forced frown on the angle of the fabric against the storm reeling beyond the windowpane. I fussed over it and stepped back until he grabbed my hand and guided me out of the room to go to sleep.

Peter fell asleep the moment his head hit the pillow, but I stared at the ceiling. My mind churned over our conversation from that evening on the foyer floor. I continued to get stuck at the point where I admitted saving that room for her, and then I would replay the conversation again. Putting the curtains on the curtain rod changed something in me, yet that statement from before echoed through my person until I fell into yet another night of nightmarish sleep...

I dreamt of disjointed places with houses standing on roofs with the plumbing pulling water from the sky and scarecrows built by gorillas in the Congo to mark their resting places. I dreamt of galaxies and forgotten things and things out of a Picasso painting that merged with Dali. I dreamt quite curiously until Seymour ripped through my designing of a constellation. It was the sound of his chuckle that turned to a cough and a smirk. I covered my ears as though caught in a stadium sound system as he chuckled again and again. His voice caused me to fall and fall and fall so quickly from my starry perch that I landed with a resounding 'thunk!' on my old porch swing at the guesthouse. I looked around, half expecting to see fairy dust rolling off of me. Who I didn't see was Seymour. I could hear his laugh coming from a window in the main house across the lawn. Smoke billowed from the chimney in what I assumed was his Saturday fire. Autumn color hung on the trees, and I was dressed in my favorite jeans with a black, shawl collar sweater from my New York days. Wait...where is the smoke coming from now? I thought as I started racing toward the house, but the lawn stretched further and further to keep the house away from me. I could see flames and three figures stumbling out of the house. I called to them, asking where the girl was.

"What girl?" came two women's voices that sounded like Seymour in falsetto.

I raced passed them and into the flames, trying to find her. I could hear a child crying, but the sound was garbled and rumbling. The heat pressed into my face and chest, but the crying grew louder and louder--

"Meeeeeeooooooooow?" I woke up with a face full of long-haired cat demon on my chest. Her tortie face cocked to one side as though laughing at me struggling to breathe. A second cry from the floor denoted another unhappy, furry member of my household. Bleary-eyed and gasping for air, I lifted the cat off my chest.

"Do you have a death wish Helvetica?" I threatened quietly while spitting out her hair from my lips and rubbing my mouth on my pajama sleeve.

She purred and swished her tail menacingly at me. I sat up, spying the 6:37 AM time on the alarm clock. Helvetica leaped onto the floor to join her cohort in crime. They sat at my feet howling like they hadn't eaten in days.

"Will you shut them up?" came a muffled voice from under a pillow.

"What do you think I'm doing?" I grumped at the lump of person wrapped in bedclothes.

"Love you" was followed by a long hairy arm patting at me from amidst the wrappings.

"Apparently someone doesn't want to be disturbed," I whispered to the cats.

They stopped their chorus when I directed my attention at them. I stumbled over them into the bathroom where I spied my jogging clothes laid neatly on the counter. I looked at the mirror to spy my reddish brown hair spiking a wicked bird's nest on top of my head. I resembled a pudgy scarecrow from my gorilla dream.

I sighed and bowed my head in defeat while the cats circled my ankles. Brutus is as big as a medium dog, so when he starts circling, I advise obedience to his whims. Either you obey or die. It is a fairly simple agreement the cats have informed me I should make. I started saying their names and asking them how many mice they saved us from while we were sleeping. I did this to distract the great sharp ones while I changed into my jogging clothes. I quickly pulled a brush through my hair to pull it into a ponytail before making my way downstairs to the kitchen.

Apparently, my slowness required quick discipline from my hellions. They ran between my footsteps like little darting hurdles of death, even on the stairs. My adrenaline still pumped from racing into a burning house, so I managed to thwart their obstacle course of doom. In minutes, they were fed, and I was stretching on the front porch for my morning jog.

The storm that raged in the evening remained a memory of yesterday. Despite the white-gold sun lazing her head above the horizon, the air had a bite to it that could only mean fall approached. I closed my eyes despite myself with autumnal tastes sneaking into every part of my person. The crisp apple and fallen leaf smells seconded my favorite smell of the stables in the fall. There is a change in the horses, the hay, and the oats that simply smells of runs through golden meadows.

Thinking about the horses sent my mind wandering to memories of Christopher. He taught me everything about horses: grooming, purchasing, racing, training, everything. Our first kiss was at the Breeder's Cup. He hadn't even placed a bet or had a horse at the race, but his enthusiasm at the win sent his lips to mine without a thought. He pulled away with those perfect lips and eyes and coiffed hair. "Now that's a win," he had said while touching my lips as though he was pressing the kiss into permanent memory. I had no words. I only smiled with delight and the feeling of being unequivocally charmed. *Oh Christopher...* My morning jog broke into a run to get away from the tears.

I started down the drive and headed toward the road away from the property. I slipped into the pace where only the thought of breathing and foot placement mattered. Breathe-step-breathe-extend further and lean-breathe...

"Morning Miss Anni!" came a voice from a car window.

Startled, I ran onto the grassy shoulder of the road. I gulped air and nodded, "Morning Mr. Thomas."

"Oh sorry. Did you not hear me coming?" Mr. Thomas slowed his ancient brown Pontiac to my pace.

I shook my head while dropping to a less-breakneck pace.

He laughed his old man guffaw. I could almost smell the stables on him despite my gasps as I ran. "Bronx Exposure foaled this morning," he stated. I nodded but still had no breath to respond. His eyes twinkled as he asked, "Miss Anni, are you trying to die like Pheidippides?"

"Who?" I managed.

"Aw Miss Anni. You've been around the world and don't know about Marathon?"

I stopped and put my hands on my knees to pant disgracefully. "Ugh, no. Maybe. I don't know, Mr. Thomas."

His amber eyes shined from his dark face, and his smile beamed. "Well, Miss Anni, it's about time you read a book," was all he said before he continued his drive home. I could hear his laughter echoing back to me.

"I do read!" I called half-heartedly to his disappearing vehicle. "I do!"

Frowning, I readjusted my ponytail and evaluated how far I had lost myself: two miles, maybe two and a half. My body was beginning to ache from the pace I had attempted. I turned back toward the house and began walking.

My mental state found itself listing through what to do when I got back home. I had forgotten that Mr. Thomas had called me late in the evening about Bronx Exposure. He usually worked late, but with a foal on the way, he slept in the tack room. He called to inform me that "Our mare is soon to foal." His leaving this morning meant that all was well, but I needed to call Dr. Oxford to make a house call to make me feel better about Bronx Exposure.

Bronx Exposure was my first horse, and her heart pounded for the race. I saw her moments after birth with wobbly legs and flashing eyes. Within minutes she raced around the stall with tail streaming. She was the first horse Christopher purchased to begin joining the ranks of the racing world. She bunked with his family's Tennessee Walking horses in a stall he designed and built himself.

Christopher missed her first race. She won and shook and huffed as though it was nothing. I raced to the winner's circle. My horse's jockey Clarence leapt off her back when he saw me, and he kissed my cheek. What the reporters didn't know is that Clarence whispered, "Christopher would be so proud of us!" The caption for the picture simply said, "Owner Annice MacKensie's eyes welling with tears and pride for Bronx Exposure and Jockey Clarence Overwood."

"If they only knew," I muttered to the empty lane and trees. It felt like a lifetime since anyone had referred to me as Annice MacKensie. Professionally, I never took on Christopher's name, so by the time that I met Peter, only the horse world knew me as a MacKensie.

I took a deep breath and sped up my walking pace to a jog. The memory of being called about Christopher's death began to play in my mind.

"No!" I said aloud to my empty path.

I broke into another run. I concentrated my entire person into every muscle and breath. I felt every footfall to the asphalt and cycle back into the air. I pumped my arms with my hands open like little daggers to cut through the air. I bent slightly forward out of good form and from childhood habit. My lungs and heart screamed to catch up, but the adrenaline laughed all the way from my toes to my scalp. At a speed that inhibited talking or thinking, I simply became *The Run*.

I ignored the magnolias lining the official drive to the house. I raced passed the columns on the front of the house and the white painted brick. I didn't stop running until I reached the tack room door in the stables. I grabbed the knob like a lifeline and swung the door open. I leaped three feet into the air and yelped despite myself.

"And good morning to you too Miss Anni," Clarence replied in Surrey overtones and his back to the door.

"Clarence Overwood, are you tryin' to give me a heart attack?" I gasped with adrenaline pumping restored through my veins.

He laughed his sparkling faerie laugh, but he didn't turn from his work oiling a saddle. "You are as loud as a horse in the last turn, or I would be asking you the same question."

I frowned at his back and pouted despite myself. "Pardon me asking, but why are you here?"

"Mr. Thomas called to inform me about Bronx's foal. He said your stable hand is gone for the weekend, so I offered to take Hunter out for a ride this morning so that Mr. Thomas could rest," Clarence paused and turned to face me. "I've been here helping him since three."

I gasped despite myself and covered my mouth. His left eye was so blackish purple and swollen that I wasn't certain he could see out of it. "Oh Clarence!" I started toward him. He held up a hand.

"It's my own fault," he stated blandly. His lips pressed together in a thin line.

I frowned again and crossed my arms. "Oh really? You punched yourself in the face?"

He smiled, but only barely, and turned back to the saddles. In the years we had known one another, I had grown used to Clarence's dramatic pauses. He weighed each word and sentence before speaking. I stifled an urge to sigh at his five foot six figure and stomp from the room. Instead, I opened my mouth and--

"I had a lapse of judgment," he said quietly while lifting my saddle and turning toward me. "Heathcliff's Final Folly misses you."

His visible blue eye bore through my person, but I didn't close my mouth. "Clarence," I seemed to sigh and spit his name, "you can't distract me with the reason I came here in the first place. What happened?"

"I had a lapse of judgment and punched myself in the face by way of another man's fist in a pub." He continued to extend the saddle toward me. His right brow arched high on his head.

I must have begun to give a tone, but all I remember is shaking my head and stamping a foot.

"Now don't start with me," he groaned and shook the saddle at me.

My eyes bore into his face. I chewed on a million things to scream at him while the memories of hiring Clarence popped into my head. I remembered meeting a very drunk Clarence after a race in a pub in New York City. Christopher and I had stopped there to meet a friend. Clarence had started a bar fight that concluded in an accidental breaking of the innocent bystander Christopher's nose. Three days later, Mr. Thomas introduced us to who should be our jockey: the man who broke his nose! Christopher trusted Mr. Thomas, and when Mr. Thomas said that Clarence was who we needed, Christopher submitted to his word immediately. Before fully committing, Christopher looked to me because Clarence would be riding my horse. "He can only jockey for us if he stays sober," I had relented, and all three men gave me their word that this was reasonable. (I found out years later that Mr. Thomas and Christopher had been holding Clarence's head over a toilet fifteen minutes preceding our meeting). Here we stood again in a face off in the stables, yet this time, Mr. Thomas and Christopher were nowhere to be found.

"Fine. I won't start with you," I grabbed the saddle from him with jerk and spun on my heel.

"I wasn't drunk Anni."

I paused mid-step out the door. "That's none of my business anymore Clarence."

He placed his hand on my shoulder and stopped me from progressing into the stables. Tears sprung to my eyes. I was beginning to believe my eyes had become motion-activated faucets.

"Don't be like that. I may not ride for you, but we're still family." I relaxed my shoulder under his hand and began to turn toward him. Clarence kissed my cheek. "I'll heal up fine. My ride this morning was just what the doctor ordered."

"How long has it been since you rode?" I asked softly.

"Since I started working for Jo Ellen's father," he shrugged.

Our eyes met, and we both nodded.

"I'm glad that Mr. Thomas called you," I half-smiled.

He smirked and released my shoulder. "Don't forget to peek in on the little one. He's going to need a name."

"He?"

"Oh yes. Something bookish or artistic knowing you," he grinned.

Nodding and smiling, I lifted the saddle at him as though I was tipping my hat before backing out the door. I turned toward the far end of the stables. I took a few steps toward the sunlight burning white outside the open stable doors. I heard Clarence move, and in my peripheral vision, I saw the door to the tack room begin to close.

"Hey Clarence? Why don't you ride with me?" I said while still gazing at the light casting a burnished haze over the training ring and trees beyond it.

The tack door hesitated. I could hear the horses stirring before me. The new foal's little hoof sounds suddenly pranced and crushed hay to my right. Dust motes filtered passed my view. I fancied the thought of Jenny riding across the meadow towards me with her dark hair streaming behind her. I pictured her at the delicate age of twelve in riding pants and a shirt she snagged from my closet. I had no picture of her at her current age of sixteen, so instead, I watched the phantasm of a child not my own wave me to ride before disappearing into the white-hot sun beams at the stable doors. Motionless and afraid to blink, I missed the tack room door open wider.

Clarence carried a saddle and blanket underneath one arm so that he could shut the door with his free hand. His free arm remained slightly crooked as the hand pulled the knob. The sound of a gasp and "bloody hell" knocked me from my thoughts. I turned to him, "You okay?"

"Mmhmm," he nodded with his bright blue eyes clouded by a furrowed brow and frown. "I'd love to ride with you."

I frowned at him while spying the lack of mobility in his right arm. The look he cast at me buttoned my lip. I nodded and began walking toward Hunter while Clarence went for one of our carriage horses that I called "Scoop."

One of the draws to using our estate for wedding bookings is our carriage option. Almost every bride who meets our black Friesian sisters Scoop and Sundae looks at whoever accompanies her and says in a girlish whisper, "Oh can we please make this happen?"

When our most recent bride Jayne toured the grounds, she looked at me with tears in her eyes and said, "Black Beauty was my favorite book growing up. May I feed them carrots?" Surprised, I pulled a few from my pockets and guided her to

Sundae. Very softly, she stroked Sundae and said, "You were in my dream wedding when I was a little girl. I'm so glad to meet you."

I glanced to Jack, my event planner. He shook his head with an almost imperceptible "no." Sundae nuzzled her cheek in hopes of another carrot, and Jayne reluctantly patted her nose while pulling herself back to her future groom Edwin. Before Jack could stop me, I was offering to do her bridal photography shoot with Sundae. "Consider it my wedding gift," I said. She began to cry and threw her arms around my neck with complete abandon. She had no words. Her future groom turned red, and his Adam's apple bobbed up and down. When they left the stables with Jack, Edwin whispered to me, "Thank you for giving her what I couldn't."

When I told Peter this story, he took one look at my face and grabbed my hand, "Let's do more." My heart soared. We called Jack that moment and changed their wedding package to include all the carriage options. Then, we plotted how to tell them at her bridal shoot with Peter dressed in our driver's livery.

"What are you thinking about?" Clarence interrupted my remembering.

"The bride from the wedding we hosted last weekend," I smiled misty-eyed to myself while I struggled to pull myself onto Hunter.

Clarence was already mounted on Scoop who was pawing the ground eagerly for a ride. The intensity of my morning run had finally hit my legs. I was on my third attempt to get good footing to swing myself up on Heathcliff's Final Folly, who we nicknamed "Hunter."

"Out of practice, eh?" Clarence chuckled at me.

I pursed my lips and narrowed my eyes at Clarence when my third attempt proved successful. Hunter huffed at me impatiently. "'C'mon Hunter," I said before making clicking noises with my tongue.

We trotted forward toward the meadow. Clarence remained at my right. "So, why are you thinking about the most recent wedding? I thought you had that event planner. Oh, what's his name? The gay one?"

I laughed, "Gay? Jack is married to a lady with three kids. His wife is a caterer. They adore weddings. He was an editor at the magazine I used to work at in New York. They moved to Nashville when I offered him this job."

Brows arched and mouth agape, Clarence stared at me. "But he's...well...frankly he's too well dressed to be straight."

He paused for effect. I began to laugh because that's the exact same thing he said about Christopher.

"You really don't understand fashion do you? I mean...jockeys always look ridiculous in races."

Clarence groaned and off he started on the history of the jockey uniform and its impact on society. I leaned slightly forward and urged Hunter to a faster pace. While continuing his jockey fashion dissertation, Clarence urged Scoop faster. I urged Hunter to break into a run to drown out the history lesson.

"Hey amateur! You can't beat a jockey!" I heard his voice call in the wind.

Clarence may be the male, athletic version of my physical self, but Scoop is not a racehorse. She thinks she is, but in actuality, Hunter is the two time Derby champion with quite a few accolades.

"Hey jockey! You're on a carriage horse!" I taunted back at him.

I don't know how long we ran. Everything disappeared except the wind and hoof beats and someone's laughter. Hunter's stride extended through his most beautiful gait. His blackish-chestnut coat gleamed with sun and sweat. The meadow streamed around me. I closed my eyes to feel the run as completely as breathing. The smell of wild flowers and meadow grass overtook me. My hair fell completely out of its bun. Mindlessly, I began to rein Hunter back and opened my eyes.

Hunter and I turned and headed back toward Clarence who was paces and paces behind us. He eased up on Scoop who was having the ride of her life. His good eye sparkled as he shook his head at me. I had forgotten his black eye, so it startled me back into reality.

"I haven't heard you laugh like that in a long time," he smiled and touched my elbow when we neared one another.

"What are you talking about? Who was laughing?"

"You were!" he smiled and shook his head at me in disbelief.

"The person laughing was me?" I laughed again, and this time it felt solid and attached to my vocal chords. "Wow that feels good. Why has it been so long?" I asked no one in particular.

I could see thunderheads moving in from the west. The pace was slow enough that I knew we had at least an hour before they would reach us. The wind had changed from my morning run, and I could smell the hail in the storm. We paused and watched a crack of lightning flash and disappear in the sheet of gray that melted and muddled the clouds from the sky into the earth.

"Why has it been so long?"

"What?" I squinted and turned toward Clarence with forgotten ease.

"You asked 'why has it been so long?' so I am asking you to answer yourself," he shrugged and looked me right in the eyes.

We held each other's gaze. His bruised eyelid struggled to show signs of life, but his good eye remained as calm and patient as the ocean. I blinked and groaned. He pumped his fist laughing.

"One good eye and I still beat you!"

"Stubborn Englishman," I muttered. "He must be part Irish."

"Oi! What did you say?" he nudged Scoop tauntingly toward me. Hunter didn't move.

"I--" I giggled.

Clarence punched my shoulder. I kicked his calf. Scoop huffed. They both gave me the stink eye. I pointed at Clarence. He pointed back, and we made angry faces at each other before busting into cackles.

"Wow," he said softly.

"Yeah?" I started to pick of the reigns and decided to twist my hair back into a bun instead of moving forward. He remained quiet while watching me. I contained my bird's nest disaster into a fairly smooth mound. I tucked away bumps and stray hairs behind ears as he cleared his throat uncomfortably.

"It's been a long time to not see you, friend," he said with a hoarse tone to his voice. He coughed and turned his eyes to the horizon.

"It has," I nodded and watched the storm hovering and extending.

He made a noise and patted Scoop. She began walking forward, so I squeezed my heels to encourage Hunter to follow. I allowed Clarence to remain slightly ahead of me with his thoughts. He sat fairly straight in the saddle with his hips and legs melting into Scoop's stride. It dawned on me then that he was wearing the blue oxford shirt I once gave him to wear to visit his mother.

The wind picked up. Trees and grass swung and bowed over one another like children on an underwater playground. Hunter's ears went back the instant a crack of lightning streaked the horizon and smacked a roll of thunder toward us.

"Where'd you go?" Clarence asked, suddenly beside me.

I jumped and gasped in the saddle. He smiled with most of his uninjured face, and I shook my head with barely a dimple showing.

"That's a loaded question these days."

"You've dealt with me loaded, so I can deal with you loaded."

I swatted at him, but he ducked while chuckling. I rolled my eyes and took a deep breath. He waited.

"You know that's not what I mean."

"I do, but you're lightening up for the first time since you moved to the estate," he paused. "I take that back. There were a couple months in there where you lightened up, but I think that had more to do with marrying Peter and you two...ya know...consummating."

"Um gross! How do you make something special sound so...business-like and ugh," I groaned.

He laughed, yet his good eye never left my face. I looked at my hands on the reins. The thunder mumbled and grumbled toward us. I turned Hunter back toward the house at a gentle pace. Clarence followed.

I felt the words rise from my core. My inner monologue's filter flung aside from the internal pressure. What came out of my mouth streamed in the worst kind of word-vomit. It erupted with the force of a geyser finally cracking through the earth's crust for the first time. My words shot and tumbled out and up to heaven while splattering across Clarence, the horses, and me. I didn't even see Clarence as I emotionally burst. I spoke while watching it happen again with the fuzzy clarity of a memory video.

I still can't believe I started it with, "I lived in a hell that I had no idea had so expertly wrapped its tentacles into and around me that I was afraid to leave. I had become a fixture in their living nightmare."

Clarence paled. His brows went into question marks. He kept his lips in a thin line and simply nodded as I continued.

At first, I attempted backtracking. The entire experience hadn't been so bad. I met Jenny my very first day. Jenny was dirt and curls and freckles and overalls. Black mud streaked in palm marks from her chest to her waist and backs of palms on her back and bottom. A smear of mud covered her forehead.

I had already gotten my keys from her mother, so I was standing on the porch to the guesthouse with my camera equipment and my red leather satchel. This mud-covered pixie appeared with spring grass colored eyes looking up at me. She opened her arms wide and embraced me without a word. I think she said that she was sorry about my husband. What I do remember is my bag falling off my shoulder and hitting the ground as she squeezed me into a hug that only children can melt their little persons into so perfectly. Tears splashed from my eyes to her head, and when she pulled away, I knew instantly she would be a frequent visitor to the house.

No, the entire experience wasn't Hell, but leaving? I looked at Clarence who nodded at me encouragingly. I swallowed.

"You never told me exactly what happened. I mean, why did you have to leave?"

"Well, the public answer is that Peter and I were getting married, and with the estate not selling, the realtor and my accountant advised that instead of spending money on a place with no people that I should actually live there and get some use out of it. I mean, I had always--what?"

Clarence had begun laughing at me. It was that dry laugh of disbelief mixed with acid that makes my skin crawl. I frowned at him, and if I had not been on a horse, I would have crossed my arms and "Harrumphed" at him.

"That explanation is about as convincing as a blank piece of paper."

"Seriously? It worked on them."

"Them? Really?"

"Yeah, I guess," I replied half-heartedly.

No explanation would have been good enough, but the giving and receiving of one was all that was necessary. If we were all honest, the real reason why I was leaving couldn't be discussed. I would have loved to go on a rampage about Seymour and Jenny and the ridiculous nature of their "relationship." It would have felt good to give everyone a piece of my mind, scoop that kid up, and both of us run to south of Franklin without looking back up I-65. I gave a few really good speeches to everyone while crying in the shower after I moved. I replayed my leaving over and over with new explanation attempts and parting words. Nothing ever fit quite as satisfyingly as the whole kidnapping scenario, but neither Jenny nor I would have seen it as a kidnapping. Of that, I am quite certain.

Rain started patting softly over us. I think Clarence yelled "C'mon" before breaking Scoop into a run. I followed after him and quickly overtook him. We barely made it into the stables before the onslaught of the storm overtook us. Laughing and breathless, we slid off the horses and chatted about the storm while we started getting the horses cleaned and settled into their stables.

*"Blue eyes and brown curls,
freckles on her face
a toothy grin and knobby knees--
She practically runs in place.*

*Long gone are overalls
and frilly, lacy dresses.
Now, she races horses
and rolls in dirt in outside spaces.*

Oh if only that were true.

(She moved today. I don't know what's going to happen to me)."

-Jenny, age 14, (diary entry)

Jenny

The phone rang and rang. I wondered what her ringer was now. When she first moved into the guesthouse, the ringer was "I Guess the Lord Must Be in New York City." She assured me that it was Sinead O'Connor's version. I blinked at her because I had no idea who "She-nayd O Con-ner" was. Later, she changed it to an antique telephone. She didn't seem as happy when it rang like that, but what did I know?

Then, she met Peter, and everything started getting better. I think she changed it to what she wanted to use for their wedding song. *What was that...?*

"Hello and thank you for calling A--"

Her voice shocked me. I gripped the phone tighter in my hand and pressed it tighter to my ear. It was actually Her. I breathed before clicking "End" on the phone receiver. *Did I cut off the voice mail? Did I just breathe into the phone? Oh no. I bet I just breathed into it like a creepy stalker. Ugh. I'm so weird. Weird and messed up.* I hit the end button on the cordless phone and dropped it.

I sat in the closet and debated over how weird and messed up I actually was. The single bulb in my walk-in closet swung above my head like a horror movie. I paused from my thoughts to stare at the bulb.

The light bounced and pushed shadows from the clothes around me and across my face. I felt like when I was little and my mother told me not to stare at the sun or I'd go blind. I stared at the bulb wishing it was the sun.

I rubbed my eyes as I stood to turn the light in the closet off. The immediate darkness felt better, safer. I sat straight back into my spot so that I wouldn't accidentally sit on the knife or phone. Had I breathed yet?

She'll call, I thought to myself. *Maybe she didn't recognize the number. Maybe I should try calling again. How long had it been?*

My sense of time was smashed. I felt like crawling under my pile of laundry and shoes. Maybe if I did then I could just become one with them.

I gulped and fumbled in the dark for the phone. My fingers grazed the knife handle. I pulled my hand back nervously and reached for the phone again. I hit a button. The phone screen lit up, so the numbers glowed. I tried not to panic while I dialed the number again.

Voice mail. Crap.

I dropped the phone in my lap without leaving a message. Please call, I hoped in my head.

The phone was on the fritz, so the time was wrong on the orange glow face. I estimated that I had been in the closet an hour, maybe two. Even in the dark, I could see his eyes burning at me in shock, but almost respect. Or was that hatred? My tongue felt like an unused sponge on the kitchen counter.

I could go get a drink from the kitchen, but it seemed risky. My mind began to race with: Did they really leave? How long will they be gone? How close is the emergency room? What kind of questions would they ask? Did I cut him deep enough?

In all of the questions, a small voice of fear began to talk to me. I hugged my knees under my chin and tried to be brave even with the very real possibility of facing his consequences. His consequences had previously included: long walks on hiking trails, all the doorknobs in the house being changed to not having locks, Anni moving, and...

Deep inside I found myself praying. I didn't know who God was or if He would even care about a girl hiding in a closet, but *Please get Anni to call me back. Please get me out of this place.*

Grandmother

The hallway hazed. I could see Seymour's figure by the door. Black dripped from his elbow as he held it bent and aloft. The light from the room cast him in shadow. The dripping had a metallic smell. I knew that smell. A voice said, "Put pressure on it." *Was that my voice?* It sounded old and quaking. *Who was that?*

I saw the glint of sunlight reflecting and bouncing on the wall before a clatter and shuffle. Seymour was saying something to the person in the room, but the voice grew louder. "We need a compress. That's too much blood."

Very little was said as I grabbed a man's handkerchief from my pocket and began to tie it on the gash. "You need to drive me to the ER. I think it's deep and will need stitches. Bring Daughter too." I nodded as he called to our daughter across the house.

We stepped together in the darkened hallway and Daughter was at the door with keys and purses. Blood was seeping through the handkerchief.

I drove the car while Daughter wrapped a towel around Seymour's arm. We raced through the winding streets to the Emergency Room. The glaring lights and smell of bleach, sweat, and paper filled our senses. Suddenly, I could see. The blood was bright. Seymour's face had gone white, and his gait fumbled through a metal detector. In minutes, we were in triage with a doctor and nurse hovering over the wound that Daughter nor I had the heart to care for well.

The nurse pulled me into the hallway because the doctor wanted a private consultation. We leaned against the wall.

"Can I get you ladies some water?" the nurse's voice squeaked like a mouse.

We both shrugged agreeably, and when she brought the water back, she cocked her head to one side as though we were now old friends and began to ask us questions. It was a futile attempt at conversation. Seymour was a retired judge. I knew plenty about when and when not to speak. I had seen the blood and direction of the "scratch" as he referred to it constantly in the car.

"But ma'am," the nurse's squeak became a demur whisper, "that's no scratch. That's a slice."

A voice responded, "If Seymour says it's a scratch, it's a scratch." The voice cracked like a rusty door hinge. Was that my voice?

Her well-manicured brows shot up and down quickly. She nodded, smiled, and checked her beeper. She excused herself to check on another patient where the sound of wild beeping echoed down the hallway.

I drank the water and looked at my daughter. She was a younger version of my blonde, pale shape. We both had green eyes, but she had Seymour's nose and mouth. We held mirror gazes for a moment before looking at the cups in our hands, like puppets moving together with identical motions. We looked at one another again and opened our mouths to speak...nothing. Without Seymour in the room, what could we say?

The doctor left with glasses on her head and her lab coat pulled tight around her. I watched her lips as she spoke softly to Seymour's nurse.

"...psychiatric consult, and be careful if you go in alone. I don't have a good feeling about this one," she whispered.

I leaned back against the wall. This was going to be a long stay.

"Ma'am?" the coffee nurse was back in front of me.

I looked at her. I'm not certain I said anything. She swallowed. "Ma'am, if you'd like, I can show you where the restroom is so that you may both wash your hands, if you'd like? The doctor has ordered a psychiatric consult. This is completely routine with this kind of injury, so you will be here for some time."

She was lying. It was sweet. My face seemed to crack and creak as I smiled at her. I looked down at my hands. I stumbled when I saw Seymour's blood covering my hands. Daughter's hands were not quite as covered. I noticed smears on her clothes were she had wiped them and bumped them while holding Seymour's compress in the car. My palms looked almost drenched with the drying remnants of his blood. Numbly, we followed the nurse to the lavatory. As a former surgeon, Daughter began to scrub to her elbows neatly and swiftly and even get under her fingernails. I watched the browned water circle in the slowed drain as I simply wrung my hands with soap and scalding water.

"Daughter," I said softly, the shock of my voice echoing across the empty stalls. "I think we should get coffee and check in with Seymour."

She nodded and replied something that got lost in the rush of the motion sensor faucet. We held one another's gaze through the mirror and didn't speak a word again for quite some time.

LUNCH
Anni

"Hey Peter! Have you started the grill yet?" I called to Peter with Clarence in tow.

"I was about to fire it up since the rain stopped!" he called back from the outdoor kitchen. "How does Lemonade Chicken sound?"

"Great!" I smilingly responded in my normal voice as we neared Peter across the lawn. He hugged me with one arm while reaching out to shake Clarence's hand.

"Long time no see Clarence! How's Jo Ellen doing?" he grinned through a few days growth of beard and then looked sternly at me. "You are soaked and now you are soaking me."

I giggled and hugged him tighter. "We were in the back pasture when the rain hit. Clarence was able to change in the tack room since he's been here all night with Mr. Thomas. Got any ideas for naming a foal? He is perfect."

Peter tried to pry me away, "He? Uh oh. Are we getting back into racing since it's a stallion?"

I grinned. "Maybe. Racing would be a change from hosting weddings and events."

He laughed and I finally let him push me away so that he could begin placing the chickens on the grill. The wet imprint of my person remained on his side. He rolled his eyes at me before turning to Clarence, "Feel like racing again?"

Clarence laughed but didn't reply. I announced I was going to shower and asked if they would call Dr. Oxford to make certain he would come check the foal. They both answered "Yes!" as I slipped into the quiet of the house. Helvetica was perched on a kitchen counter. I scooped up the thirty-ish pounds of fur, which sent her into a combination growl and purr. "You aren't allowed on the counters you fur ball," I scolded while she squirmed and spun. I dropped her with a thud, and she howled at me before skulking through the foyer to sleep on a patch of sunlight. It was her fault. I would have brought her upstairs to snuggle in my bed.

Apparently Brutus preemptively read my mind and sprawled his feline self across the twisted sheets on the unmade bed. The master bedroom was a disaster. A basket of laundry was on the bed, but it was turned to the side with the clothes twisted around into a tornado. Peter's socks and boxers were across the floor leading to the bathroom. Muttering to myself, I began refolding clothes, putting them away, and picking up the various laundry items from the floor. The clothes leading to the bathroom reminded me to look at myself. I was still in running clothes with the stink of sweat and horses. Tentatively, I lifted my arm and smelled at my shoulder.

"Ugh. Oh that's terrible," I said while making a sour face at the red tub.

Shortly before moving into the estate, I had an old photography friend, Tiff, stay with me. Our friendship began when I worked as photography editor. After I retreated to Nashville following Christopher's death, she bolstered her way to the top of the art scene in New York. Her cutting edge shows utilized found objects as a component to her developing process and display. She came to Nashville to beg me to do a show with her in Paris for a gallery she knew that I would "J'adore" as much as she "J'adored it." Barely listening to her pleadings, I gave her the tourist version of Nashville, which included showing her what a "honky tonk" really was. As we rounded out our weekend, she asked me to take her to the estate.

When we walked through the front door, she gasped and began talking of all the things I could do to make the house my own. I didn't really hear her until we were standing in the master bathroom.

"The best feature in this room is the claw-footed tub. Wouldn't it just be rad to do something wild and paint the outside of it red?" she had said. Tiff always says things like "rad," and it makes me want to follow her suggestion even more.

I reached into the shower and turned it on as hot as I could stand it. Then, I peeled off my clothes while longingly staring at the tub. If Clarence wasn't downstairs with Peter, I would spend half the day in that gorgeous red tub forgetting yesterday and half my life. "Tonight there will be bath salts," I promised myself while stepping into the shower.

Everything seemed to slip down the drain: our fight, Seymour, the memories, the horseback ride, my career, everything. I started singing "Amazing Grace" in my best American Idol voice with as many dips, scats, and ridiculous additions I could manage. I barely made it through the first line before I was laughing and dancing. Steam was filling the bathroom. I decided to shampoo twice and condition my hair, so I started singing a song from an old musical about washing stuff out of my hair. I couldn't remember all the words, so I kept repeating the chorus or "watermelon" for fun.

I caught a glimpse of the suds circling the drain. It reminded me of my first trip to Milan and the old woman I saw scrubbing her cafe floor on her hands and knees. She reminded me of my grandmother with her silvery hair twisted in a bun but stray pieces falling in her face. She was pushing sudsy water with a coarse brush and great vigor. Her forearms rippled in feminine strength. Without thinking, I crouched in the street and took her picture. She looked up, and I accidentally snapped another one. She yelled in exasperation at me for loitering and being a stupid American tourist. Quietly, I rushed to her with as many Italian apologizes that I could muster and remember. I kneeled beside her to explain that she was so beautiful being herself that I couldn't help but take a picture. Her face brightened as she informed me that I had a very good accent and should eat breakfast with her. I took the floor brush from her, kissed her cheeks, and said that I would be honored. A swirl of suds nestled around our knees in a picture only my memory kept. Then, she fed me the best meal I have ever eaten in Italy. She helped me with my Italian and I helped her with her English. We laughed about fashion, and she showed me pictures of when she was a model.

"My daughters, very beautiful, always asked to model, but now they have lots of babies. No time to model," she said proudly. "So many babies, and all work here."

I met all her family as they stumbled in to begin prepping for lunch. Their arms were full of fresh ingredients. Her eyes sparkled, and for the first time since I moved to New York, I missed home. While everyone bustled in the kitchen, I moved to the forgotten bucket and plunged the brush into it. I picked up where Adalina had stopped and began finishing the floor. I allowed their chatter to turn into Italian music around me instead of attempting to translate their conversation for myself. Then, out of nowhere, strapping, hairy arms encircled my waist and pulled me to my feet.

"Bella no no no no no no!" came the deepest, sexiest voice I had ever heard. The bucket got kicked which sent suds and water arching across the floor and into the street. The brush flew out of my hand toward the door. I gave a most unfeminine grunt. Everyone in the family was laughing at us.

"Francesco!" his sister chided him and picked up the bucket. Someone else fetched the brush. I was placed in a chair, handed a glass of wine, and a sliver of cheese was shoved into my mouth. "Eat, no work!" Adalina wagged her finger at me, and soon, she and her children were regaling me with stories of terrible customers, tourists, and a rivalry among the bakers. The memory disappeared like another snapshot in my camera.

In the shower, I fought the urge to touch the suds swirling around the drain. Instead, I grabbed my washcloth and a mostly unused bottle of body wash. I frothed the body wash onto the cloth into a million bubbles and blew some of them at the glass door. I giggled to myself and began to lather.

As I rinsed the mounds of bubbles, I sang, "I'm gunna wash that job right outta my hair." I stopped and mentally stepped away from myself. What had I just said? All at once, I knew exactly what I had to do. I began lathering, rinsing, and singing away all the memories I wanted gone. I washed memories of me getting teased as a kid on the playground and of my first rejected concept for work. I let go of bad ideas, negative reviews, and horrible grades. I sang and laughed while imagining all of it slipping down the drain never to return to me. The water was beginning to turn cold, and I hadn't let go of everything. I turned the hot knob higher and rinsed my face again. The jets of water traced my face. I reached out and braced myself against the wall.

The last time I stood like that ended with me in a ball in my Manhattan apartment tub crying because Christopher was dead and never coming home. I refused to end up in a ball again, especially over things I couldn't change, so I stood there. I stood there trying not to breathe the water while the bubbles on the glass door slowly disappeared with the soap bubbles down the drain.

The water went cold. I turned it off and stepped out of the shower to grab my towel. My cell phone rang in the pocket of my running pants, but I ignored it. I decided it must be Peter calling to let me know lunch was ready, which was strange because he rarely rushed me on Saturdays. I shook my head as I toweled my tingly skin.

I turned the bathroom fan on and wiped the fog from the mirror. For a second I didn't recognize myself. My face looked full and pink, yet the circles under my eyes made me look perpetually tired.

Still, I looked...different. *Was that peace peeking in the light twinkles in my eyes, or maybe it was just the light fixture reflection?*

"--NCH," I heard calling from a muffled distance.

I waved off what I thought was Peter's call. Instead, I leaned forward closer into the mirror. The imaginary helmet of shame had melted away, and my skin actually looked lighter. I smiled and checked my teeth. Standing straighter, I took a deep breath. "Wow. I'm me again," I sighed in relief. How long had it been?

"--nni! Lunch!"

Quickly, I tousled my hair with curling product before throwing on a sundress that I had missed in my quick laundry sweep of the room. I was halfway down the stairs in my bare feet before realizing the last time I wore this particular sundress. I genuinely thought I had burned that dress along with half a dozen pictures and a wooden cigar box Seymour had given me. Then the realization hit me square in the face. I stumbled. My stomach leapt to my throat, but I kept pressing forward. I last wore it *that* day.

"I let that go in the shower," I muttered determinedly at the memories attempting to flood back in my ears and across my eyes.

The images stopped.

"Lad I don't know where ya been but I see ya won first prize!" a familiar voice filled my mind before I could be bombarded by memories again. Peter and Clarence were laughing. Peter said something, but it was muffled as I reached the patio door in the kitchen. Clarence's wife Jo Ellen stood by the kitchen door.

"Well hello Jo Ellen! I'm so glad you could join us," I found myself saying genuinely and holding my arms out to her for a sisterly embrace.

She hugged me and patted the middle of my back three times before releasing me. I glanced at Peter and flicked three fingers quickly at him. He smiled at our private joke. People who hugged like Jo Ellen caused us to wonder if they really meant their hugs or simply gave it a "One, two, three" boxing count to make certain that the hug went down long enough for everyone involved.

Surprisingly, this time Jo Ellen grabbed my hand like an old friend as she turned back to Clarence.

"Oh Anni, I haven't seen ya or tha house in ages, and I was soooo glad y'all invited us to lunch with y'all. I was just tellin' the boys that I'd loooove to see how ya finished redoin' the place for weddin's. Mind givin' me a tour?" she smiled at Clarence the entire time she spoke before turning back to me for the answer.

I blinked at the shock of her blue eye shadow. For the first time I realized she had fallen into the recent catastrophe of the eighties revival, but with her own interpretation. She had even included a penciled lip freckle, glittered her eyes, and worn a neon pink and black plaid shirt. As an artist, I could see the spectacle and wonder of the 80s with its flashy, almost reinterpreted Baroque quality, but the resurgence was beyond my taste. At least she looked...authentic with her frosted hair in a messy bun.

"Oh um, well, I guess that depends on the chickens. Peter?" I looked at him with brows up, praying he could read my eyes.

"We have about twenty to thirty minutes left. I was about to recruit Clarence inside to help me with some home fries and sides when Jo Ellen came in," Peter smiled smugly.

I was trapped. Jo Ellen clapped her hands and jumped up and down before grabbing my hand again. "It's settled. Let's start at the front door and work our way through. I want to know about everything and all about the weddings you've hosted."

I tried not to sigh. I had a feeling she was more interested in who used the grounds for weddings than the Degas hanging in the Bridal Suite or Ansel Adams in the Groom Suite or the *Dali Atomicus* print by Halsman I hoarded in my studio. (I find those to be the most appealing stories in the house, but as Peter often reminds me, not everyone wants an art history lesson in a home tour). She paid no attention to my expression while half dragging me through the house so that we could stand on the front steps and I could introduce her to the house. While her delight was contagious, did she really care why I chose a slate blue for the main foyer?

We stood on the gravel drive and looked up at the front of the house. I took a deep breath, gestured to the house with a sweeping hand, and said, "Welcome to the Keystone House. The house was built by my first husband's great-great-grandfather before it partially burned. His great-grandfather rebuilt it, but it was his grandfather who actually expanded and completed the home in the architecture and design as you see it now."

Jo Ellen nodded seriously as we walked up the steps. She practically vibrated when I pushed the heavy wooden door open. She pulled the scarf from around her neck and clutched it in her hands like a fabric bouquet as she entered the foyer. Slowly, she stepped to the middle of the floor and turned in a gentle circle. She scrutinized every inch from floor to ceiling silently. When she finished, her first question was:

"So why American Walnut and are the window panes original?"

A terrible actress, I didn't even attempt to hide my surprise. Instead, I sputtered some response and got tongue-tied before starting over with the real answer. She listened intently and then began to ask other pointed questions about the staircase, slate blue paint, and floor plan. My heart soared. This kind of home tour might include an art history discussion! (I had grossly underestimated her).

Delighted yet serious, we entered and discussed every room in the house. I found myself telling her about the pieces the old butler cried over that I asked him to take and the Ming vase everyone in Christopher's family fought over until I told them I was keeping it with the house.

"That niche here in the relaxing room was custom designed to fit that specific vase," I gestured to it.

To which Jo Ellen appropriately replied, "And you cain't just run about all willy-nilly lookin' for some vase that might could fit in that nitch because it just might not be a good enough color or size."

"That's what I said. Sort of," I smiled. She beamed.

We continued out to the old kitchen, which I had turned into my studio. The original kitchen to the house burned down completely, so my now current studio was in the kitchen built by Christopher's grandfather or great-grandfather around 1900 or 1912.

"I'm fuzzy on the details, but what I do know is that whoever rebuilt it put in higher ceilings, lots of windows, and a much, much bigger hearth," I smiled and opened the door.

Jo Ellen barely made it in the door before she gasped. The fireplace took up an entire wall. I had outfitted anew the entire inside with new walls, floors, electricity, plumbing, everything. I added some space to the back of the studio so that I could retrofit a bathroom and add a traditional darkroom.

"It's so bright," she said and walked toward each photograph hanging on the walls before turning her attention to the farm table I used as my main work surface.

Lying in an oversized frame on my desk was a picture of a woman in a crimson gown with a long piece of matching fabric flinging toward the camera. She was flipping backward, almost as though doing aerial acrobatics. In all truth she had been laughing and tripped, which sent her into a reflexive back handspring. I had the camera going and happened to catch this shot.

"She didn't catch herself as gracefully as the shot might lead you to believe," I confided and opened my laptop to show her the archived footage I kept from the shoot.

"Wait, you mean she didn't do this on purpose?" Jo Ellen's eyes were wide.

"Oh no, but it was one of those moments that we happened to catch. It's similar to this shot I did with her later that year but from a different angle," I pulled up the unused files and showed her the series of Edda flying backward and landing in the arms of two strapping Italian assistants. "Needless to say, Edda married that one that did most of the catching. His name is--no joke--Tito."

"Tito! I looooove it," Jo Ellen looked up at me with shining eyes. I noticed that they were actually a dark blue-gray. It suddenly made the blue eye shadow not seem so stark.

"Right? Soooo Italian," I laughed. I was starting to talk like her. How long had we been touring? I glanced at the clock on the laptop. "Oh goodness. I bet Peter and Clarence have already split one of the chickens by now! We should hurry back."

"I guess we should," she agreed and reluctantly set the photograph back on the table. "I just have one question. Where are ya thinkin' of hangin' the picture?"

I looked at her rather sheepishly, "Well, remember how I have a red tub in my bathroom?"

Her laugh twinkled like violins. With her head back and hand touching her stomach, I caught a glimpse of what Jo Ellen must have looked like as a child. Her laughter softened every feature. Without thinking, I reached out for my camera on the table.

"I looooove it."

We walked back to the patio arm in arm. I carried my camera. For a moment, I experienced a weird sense of déjà vu as Peter and Clarence came into view on the back porch, yet it wasn't déjà vu. It felt familiar: walking arm in arm, the smell of grilled chicken, and the sound of thunder...

"Hey ladies, how was your tour?" Peter called to us. Being the taller of the two, he saw us first.

"A de-light," Jo Ellen called back while keeping her brisk pace.

I swallowed and brightly yelled, "Total blast. She loves the photograph for the bathroom!"
I heard him groan and mutter something to Clarence who chuckled mischievously. Peter was in the middle of plating lunch. Clarence stood and kissed his wife before ushering her over to the table. She immediately began regaling him with all the details of the house. I hurried over to help with the plates.

"I'm glad you two had fun. I tried calling you, but it just rang and rang, so I guessed when you two might finish after I saw you leave the house toward the studio," he spoke softly with his eyes never leaving his work.

"You called?" I asked perplexed. "I'm sorry you've called me so much this morning and I haven't answered."
I slipped my arm around his waist as he finished the final plate. He hugged me and kissed my forehead. "I haven't called you all morning my love. I just called you the once."

I felt my forehead scrunch and my lips frown. Out of the corner of my eye I saw Clarence gesturing something I could only guess was the size drink she would want. He hurried to the kitchen as Peter and I carried the plates to the table.

"Well don't ya just beat all! This looks even better than edible Peter," Jo Ellen grinned ear to ear.

We all laughed and agreed. Clarence reappeared with glasses and a pitcher on a tray.

"What is this?" my eyes arched in surprise. Peter chuckled beside me while we took our seats. I looked from one smug face to the other. "Well?"

"I know how much you love sangria..." Peter trailed off.

Jo Ellen clapped her hands in delight. "I love it too! We never drink it because," she glanced at Clarence and then at her hands, "well, we just don't."

"It's non-alcoholic wine Jo," Clarence smiled at her while distributing glasses.

"So it's grape juice sangria?" she looked up at him with scrunched brows and an upturned lip.

"Gross," she and I chorused together.

Grandmother

Daughter guided me to the hospital cafeteria in silence. We purchased coffee that tasted and smelled like tar. No amount of cream and sugar could save it. I should have purchased sweet tea.

As we reentered Seymour's room, his eyes went directly to my cup. I handed it to him and said, "We got this for you." He smiled and said thank you to Daughter first and then me. Then his eyes cut to another person in the room.

The man seemed to appear out of the wall: thin build, pale skin, tan suit, white shirt, yellow tie, brown shoes. He may as well have been the privacy curtain. He extended a limp, soft hand as he introduced himself, "Please. Call me John."

"It's a pleasure," the three of us chorused.

"John is doing a mental status evaluation due to the nature of my cut," Seymour looked deep into my eyes. I understood and nodded.

"Well I don't understand why it's even necessary. It was an accident," I felt my voice bubble in my throat as I held his gaze.

"That's what I said, but hospital protocol is hospital protocol," he didn't blink, but he held his forefinger tip to his thumb on his good hand, just like you would when holding a string.

I glanced at his hand before looking at the wisp of a man named John. "We can step out of the room while you discuss with him what happened, but I assure you. It was an accident. He would never inflict harm on himself." Then I looked at Daughter. Her gaze had sunk into the floor.

Seymour sank into his pillow and nodded at me. "Will you give Mackendrick Sheffield a call for me to speed this hospital process along? I know he'll be delighted to hear how well everyone is treating us here."

I nodded as John said, "Ah so you know our favorite magistrate."

Seymour smiled and closed his eye, "Sure do. I topped his daddy in law school and helped Lil Mack get his current seat. I've heard his daddy talk about sitting on the board of the children's hospital now. Is that true or is he pullin' my leg?"

John swallowed so hard his Adam's apple bobbed like a puck on a high striker game at the fair. His diplomatic response was, "I'm not sure but I can certainly look into for you to know for your next golf game."

Seymour laughed. "Poker son. High stakes."

Daughter and I melted out of the room as Seymour's new friend chuckled nervously. The nurse from earlier was on her way in to check Seymour's blood and fluid levels. She smiled at me as she pushed a computer cart bigger than she was.

"Would you be more comfortable in the waiting room for the time being? I know there aren't many chairs in there, and we'll be in and out until the doctor discharges your husband," she smiled warmly. "I can get you a coffee or hot tea? The cafeteria coffee is abysmal."

I laughed in agreement. "Actually I could use a phone with an outside line access. We raced out and forgot our mobile phones. I just realized we need to check to see if my granddaughter is home and can take the dog for a walk."

I could feel Daughter tense. Neither of us had spoken of Jenny. She silently walked away and tossed her untouched coffee cup into a trash can by the nurses' station.

"Well of course ma'am! It's down the hallway to your left by the bathroom. It isn't completely private, but it will be quieter than the waiting room at this time of day," she beamed. "Now time to check everything!"

Daughter and I slipped to the phone so that I could call Mackendrick Sheffield, just as Seymour asked. The call went straight to voicemail, so I left him a short message before calling his father. Retired like Seymour, Cartwright Sheffield kept his fingers in numerous pies around the city. Of the Boston Sheffields, Cartwright moved to Nashville under Seymour's prodding to start their own firm. I remember the first time he stepped off the train while Seymour was still courting me. He wore a black knee-length traveling coat and gray homburg hat. Even in retirement, the cleft in his chin and ruddy cheeks looked best beneath that homburg. He was recently wed to Matilda, whom he called Tilly. She emerged from the train in a stylish camel colored traveling coat with a sapphire blue dress peeking from beneath it. When she died a few years earlier of cancer, Cartwright made certain his Tilly wore a blue that would have matched her eyes. His voice startled me from the memories, and I responded kindly who and where I was.

"Well my dear woman, I must put a stop to this game right now. I tell you I am three strokes behind and getting worse with every hole. You are saving me, and I'm delighted to help get Seymour out and resting at home. Tell him that he will owe me a better seat at the poker table next game," Cartwright's easy laugh erupted in my ears as though I was hearing joy in laughter for the first time.

"I will Cartwright. Please tell Mackendrick we left him a message as well since we didn't want to bother you at the club."

"Of course madam. I'll be in touch."

He clicked off the phone as I turned to see that Daughter was slipping into the bathroom. I hung the phone on the hook and leaned against the wall to wait for her. Voices drifted toward me from conversations that barely made sense. I was still lost on that train platform all those years ago with Seymour in his fedora and suit as he stood next to Cartwright.

"...the best call Regina. He's a former judge, so he'd be far more suspicious if we were throwing two police detectives at him. The story is an accident, but those scratch marks are questionable."

I perked up and moved to the other wall where I could hear more clearly.

"With all the loss of blood, I don't think he's realized the other scratch marks because the only one he refers to is the knife wound, and it's somewhat deep for a slip and fall accident."

"We'll see what John says. He'll know how to proceed. They were laughing like old friends as I left from taking stats, so hopefully inhibitions are lowered with the blood loss."

The bathroom door opened which caused me to jump. Daughter started to speak but I held a finger to my lips as I turned to listen more. The nurses' conversation was cut short by a beep at the nurses' station and lights blinking. I could hear footsteps racing. We slipped from our alcove in the Emergency Department and carefully made our way back to Seymour's room as we avoided some running nurses and attending physicians going the opposite direction of us. When we reentered the room, both men were in deep political debate about the current state congressmen and governor. Seymour held up a hand and cleared his throat as we entered.

"How was Mackendrick?"

"Actually, Cartwright is stopping his golf game to handle this situation. The moment the doctor discharges you, he'll be asking for a better seat at the game next Saturday."

Seymour's brows arched and he attempted to cross his arms. The I.V. prevented him, so he rested his arms back by his sides. "Old Cartwright. Did he talk your ear off per usual?" Seymour chuckled and turned his attention back to John.

"That man always had an eye for pretty women and talked them until they turned blue. His wife Tilly, God rest her soul, was a vision in blue, and he encouraged her to wear it often."

John chuckled amiably and responded, "Ah so what color would you say your wife is a vision in, sir?"

Seymour put on his politician smile that made constituents feel warm, but I knew full well that his teeth were on edge. "Oh she doesn't need to wear color. She is her own vision."

Furrowing his brows at that response, John looked to me, slightly smiled and said, "Really? With your green eyes I would have guessed green or blue might be your signature color."

"Ah only a good Southern boy knows about a woman's signature color," I felt myself smile, almost pityingly at him.

He grinned. "Born and raised ma'am."

I looked at Seymour. "Born and raised Seymour. He's practically family."

With that, I knew whatever efforts the nurses were making to keep Seymour would be thwarted. He absently rubbed his eyes as though a tired little boy. I saw the scratches the nurse mentioned when I was eavesdropping in the hallway. My heart leapt to my throat. It was as though déjà vu set into my person from when Seymour and I were first married.

I swallowed, unable to go back to that memory fully. A sudden thought triggered deep in my core, "Had he continued all these years?"

I suddenly felt fully myself. I looked at my daughter beside me. Her vacant eyes echoed the trauma that we had experienced as well as the horror that finally brought us to this hospital. It was then I began to formulate a plan.

I motioned for Daughter to follow me out of the room while the men talked. I leaned over the nurses' desk and said, "We are leaving to get some lunch. We'll be back in an hour but we don't have phones in case you need us."

The nurse smiled and said that she understood. She explained what was within walking distance if we so chose to leave.

We did so choose.

AFTERNOON
Anni

"Who wants coffee?" Peter stood while we all laughed. Peter rubbed his hands together and began stacking the plates.

"Oh me!" I smiled and started to stand.

"Jo Ellen? Clarence?" Peter asked.

They nodded up at Peter. He tapped my shoulder with his elbow and shook his head at me. I sat back down slowly. He whispered, "I got this."

"I'll help clear the table," Jo Ellen piped up.

"No no. I've got it," Peter smiled warmly.

I watched him go while Jo Ellen grabbed Clarence's chin. "Now Anni, have you ever seen such an eye?"

"What?" I looked back at them, obviously distracted by Peter's form heading into the kitchen alone. I blushed caught.

Clarence smirked at me, but Jo Ellen missed it. "I'm just sayin' that Clarence's beautiful face is just an ugly mess with this bruise."

I smirked back at him, "It is an ugly mess of a face."

Clarence's jaw dropped, but Jo Ellen cut him off before he could snap a come-back at me, "Right? I tell ya. If he had come home with this face last night, he may as well have slept in the barn."

"Oh? You came straight here?" I leaned forward.

Clarence blushed. "Mr. Thomas had called while I was out, so I decided to just come straight here to help."

Before Clarence could dig his hole any deeper, Peter reappeared with coffee mugs, creamer, and sugar. Clarence grabbed the empty sangria pitcher and glasses. Jo Ellen laughed at him, "So I guess this is you avoiding something?"

"Exactly," he kissed her forehead and headed into the kitchen.

Peter followed him with the serving dishes after a quizzical look at me. I mouthed "Later" before turning back to Jo Ellen who had started in on a story of Clarence avoiding their parents at Christmas.

I barely listened, but nodded and made appropriate noises. The conversation about Peter calling once had bubbled up in my mind again. Then it dawned on me.

"I'm sorry to interrupt you Jo, but what's the date?"

"The fifteenth, why?" she shook her head and leaned forward.

"Oh no! I left my phone upstairs and there's a wedding up at the other house!" I stood up abruptly, knocking my chair backward. I began muttering, "Shoot where did I leave my phone?"

She stood up with me, "Oh no! Wait? Other house?"

I was hurrying toward the back door. "Yeah, we bought the adjacent property to bail out the neighbors in the economic crisis in '08, and I turned their house into the main event hall for interior weddings and receptions."

"I'll help you look!" I heard her exclaim from behind me.

"C'mon!" I said, leaving the back door open.

I could hear her give some explanation to Peter and Clarence as her footsteps thundered behind me.

"Who would be calling you from the other house?" she asked from behind me.

"Our event coordinator Jack. He handles everything. He and his wife ran a full events business in New York before moving down here when I offered him the job. She now paints and sculpts while he runs events for us. We are booked almost every weekend of the year," I replied over my shoulder in our sprint. I narrowly missed the sleeping Helvetica who was sprawled on one of the stairs. Brutus was stretching in the middle of the hallway in front of my room. I leaped over Brutus only to trip and sprawl. Jo Ellen caught up with me.

"Your cats are--pardon my French--dang right huuuuuuuuge," Jo Ellen helped me the rest of the way to my feet.

"Yeah," I sputtered hair out of my mouth. I cast a dirty look at Brutus who had begun innocently bathing himself at my feet.

"Aw right. Let's find you that phone," Jo Ellen smiled and marched toward my bedroom.

"I'll start in the bedroom if you want to look around in your bathroom?" Jo Ellen suggested. "Or visa versa?"

" That's great," I agreed. "I'll retrace my steps in the bathroom."

When I got in the bathroom, I started rethinking through getting ready for the shower and then hearing my phone, *which was where?*

"Your pants!" Jo Ellen called from the bedroom.

I re-entered the bedroom to see Jo Ellen holding the phone triumphantly toward me. "That's right! I left my phone in the pocket!"

She beamed. "So, how many missed calls?"

"Three," I frowned. "But why wouldn't he call the house?"

"Who?"

" Jack, my event coordinator," I continued frowning. Only one number was listed as Peter. The other two were the same number. It looked so familiar. "No voice mails."

"Wrong number?" she suggested.

"--ffeeeeeee," I heard from downstairs.

"The coffee's ready. I won't worry about it," I shrugged and slipped the phone into my pocket again.

"We're coming!" Jo Ellen called, exaggerating the "g" sound.

"Thanks for helping. I'm glad we averted a crisis," I smiled helpfully at Jo Ellen who in turn beamed at me.

"Me too. Aside from the demon cats, I think we're safe."

"That's what I call them!" I chuckled in surprise.

We giggled together and linked arms as we walked down the stairs. She began telling me about her love/hate relationship with her mother's white Persian. A scrunched face, long-haired beauty, Jo Ellen's childhood job was daily brushing out "Muffy's mane."

"After the third attack, Mama finally took back the job from me because I was 'wraslin the cat too much,' " Jo Ellen sighed. "I swear that cat sticks her tail and hiney up at me every time I enter the room. She tears up my pillows. We had to hide all my shoes or she'd tinkle in them. Ugh. They're all evil I tell you."

"Was there an emergency? Because Jack never called down here or my cell phone?" Peter asked while pouring coffee into the mugs on the patio table.

"No. Just some number I didn't recognize," I unlinked arms with Jo Ellen so that I could pull the phone out of my pocket. "Do you recognize it?"

He didn't even bother to glance at it. "You know I am terrible with phone numbers."

"I know, but would you?" I continued holding the phone at him when it started to ring.
Startled, I looked at the screen. It was the number from earlier.

.

Jenny

I didn't know who else I could call. She was the only person who could fathom what happened. By the second ring, I was panicking. *Was she avoiding my call? Oh no! I hadn't thought of that. What if she was avoiding us and that's why we haven't talked? Wait, that can't be right because my mother---*

"Hello?"

I froze. Her voice hadn't changed. (*What had I expected*)?

"Hello?"

My left hand flew to my throat as if it could remove the weeping rock from my throat.

"Is someone there? Hello?"

My voice broke free at full volume, "Can you come get me right now?"

The phone shook in my hand. I hunched around it and cupped my hand near the receiver. I heard a shifting and silence. *Did she know it was me? Did she remember me? Did I just yell in her ear? Ugh. I'm so...*

She cleared her throat, "Can you talk?"

I quieted my voice. "No."

"Are you home?"

I sighed in relief. She had recognized the number. "Technically."

"So home isn't home?" I heard her smile amidst an avalanche of shuffling, muffled voices, and tears. Maybe the tears were mine...

"Not anymore."

"When your mom asks, tell her you called me. Don't be afraid."

"They're at the hospital. I'm in the closet."

"I'm not knocking."

"Okay."

"See you in fifteen minutes."

"But you live--"

"I'm not discussing my driving with you. Fifteen minutes soon enough?"

"Sure."

She said good-bye and told me to be brave, like before she moved.

I was finished with being brave. I felt a knot rise from my stomach and contort in my throat. I hugged my knees to my chin and placed the phone by the butcher knife to my right. The denim of my jeans was growing darker and wetter. I barely noticed. I tried to breathe normally and relax against the wall instead of thinking about memories of why the knife rested beside me.

The phone beeped. I jumped and nervously grabbed the receiver wondering who could be calling. The screen flashed the words "Charge Low Battery." Then, a blinking shape of a battery with no bars filled my vision. I turned the receiver over and yanked the battery out of it so that no one would hear me or the phone. Quietly, I place the battery and phone on the floor. Three other receivers were dismantled and piled on my laundry. My mother had wanted to sleep, so I happened to have all the receivers in my room. Anni would call it "providence." I just felt relieved.

My fingers grazed the knife handle. We had become wary allies, but soon I could leave it. Soon, I wouldn't need to keep it in my nightstand. This wooden-handled, perfectly sharp knife had stowed away in my nightstand ever since Anni moved from the guesthouse to her dead husband's estate. I was too nervous to keep it under my pillow. The nightstand seemed like a worthy, close house for the only viable ally left in my life.

Knives could be trusted, but locks couldn't. I had tried depending on them when Anni moved. I wanted to sleep without fear hovering in my room like bats in a cave. At first, keeping the door locked worked. I remember hearing the knob start to turn and pulling the covers over my head. The knob jiggled. I heard quiet words that I wasn't allowed to use and then my name. I woke up the next morning to blueberry pancakes and my daddy in the kitchen! I raced over to him while he was pouring more batter on the griddle. It spilled in a long line. He laughed at me and said that I just made him a rectangle pancake. A muffled yell came from he and my mother's bedroom. Daddy lowered his voice and winked while telling me to watch the pancakes because he wanted to surprise my mother with a stack. Nobody knew that Daddy was home.

I watched the edges of the rectangle pancake bubble and start to turn brown. Suddenly, hands were on my shoulders and all my joy evaporated into a silent scream in my throat. The voice in my ear was ever so soft, "Think you can keep your door locked do you?" I nodded, and then my daddy came in the kitchen.

Daddy greeted him, "Mornin' Seymour."

We all called him Seymour. I don't know why he was never "Grand-daddy" or "Papaw" like other kids called their grandfathers. When Daddy appeared, Seymour let go of my shoulders and held out his hand to shake my daddy's hello.

Seymour and my grandmother ate breakfast, but they hurried back home to their farm, much to my relief. Like usual, Daddy's appearance at home was short. He disappeared around midnight with the bag he kept packed in the closet.

A day or so later after Daddy left, Seymour and my grandmother appeared with large suitcases and a box of crystal doorknobs with brass plates. He showed the box to my mother saying, "I know you haven't found knobs you preferred for all the doors since you renovated, and I thought you might like these better."

She clapped her hands together like a toy monkey with cymbals. "Why don't you help me?" he said to me. We worked quietly starting with my mother's room and went through the rest of the house. We ended the silent day at my bedroom. I remember him speaking for the first time as he pulled the old knob out of the door that Anni had helped me install before she moved.

"Don't think I don't know who helped you with this," he had said softly. I was holding the new knob while he screwed it in place with a Phillips head screwdriver.

I didn't respond.

"Just remember," he continued in a sing-song whisper," you are my flesh and blood. Not hers. She has no claim over you like I do."

I remember backing away, forgetting my hold on the knob and plate. His snake black eyes bore into me.

"And don't forget that I can kill you or your mother and no one would know it was me...no one would find you. I was a state's attorney and a judge. I know what to do, so you better not tell."

I still tremble thinking about what he said next, "But you know I don't have to do that. I'm all talk-- just a teddy bear, especially when you are obedient."

I blinked. The memory of his face disappeared, and I was alone in the closet. The darkness kept the sight of closet knob away from me. I was gripping the butcher knife, my last remaining ally.

Shortly after the locks changed, Seymour began taking me on outings more often, far away from the knife in my room. It wouldn't surprise me if he had found it. Still, the bedroom was my last safe place. I tried every excuse. I hid there doing homework, often with the knife in my lap. I joined every school group activity and project possible to keep me in that room because I knew he feared being caught again in the house.

I swallowed and tried to guess at the time. Then it dawned on me: Anni was on her way. I had made sure she still had a key to the house. She would have a way in even if Seymour and my grandmother had locked the door on the way to the hospital. When Seymour changed the doorknobs inside the house, he told my mother that she needed new exterior knobs to better match the interior.

"I'll pay and do it myself. Consider it a birthday gift, just from your daddy," he practically purred at her. I wanted to vomit.

I had listened in on his phone order for the knobs. "Yeah Larry. I do want those knobs we talked about and the extra keys made," he had called from Daddy's office. The brass knobs were $144 each with a very specific type of key. Thank goodness that the maid was given a master key to the house for access to certain locked closets, so I swiped one of two spare keys meant for her. I mailed it to Anni from school. The school secretary didn't bat an eye when I made an excuse about mailing something for my mother. Everyone knew about her "delicate condition." I tucked the key in a card that said, "Just in case. Jenny." The key was labeled master, so not even a deadbolt could keep her out. I just hoped that in two years she had kept the key.

I could hear footsteps coming down the hall, but I wasn't going to check to see who it was. I heard the bedroom door creak open.

DESSERT
Anni

"You're white as a sheet," Clarence spoke first after I clicked "end" on my mobile phone.

Clarence, Jo Ellen, and Peter stood in a semicircle in front of me. I felt like I was moving in slow motion.

"This can't be really happening?" I think I said out loud.

"Where do you need to be in fifteen minutes Anni?" Peter said from beside me.

I looked toward the kitchen door. "I told her I'd be there in fifteen minutes. You finish the coffee and dessert without me. I'll be back in about an hour."

"What? Have you lost it?" Peter grabbed my arm as I attempted to walk to the door. "Who was on the phone?"

"It was Jenny," I felt my voice grow stronger, more real. This wasn't a dream. It wasn't the recurring nightmare of a child caught in the house on fire. It wasn't the flashbacks to the latter part of the year after I caught them in the guest bedroom and everyone continued to deny the truth. This was real and something very bad had happened. Jenny wouldn't call out of the blue unless it was bad.

"I'm coming with you. Where's that key she mailed you? The one with the filigree on the end?" Peter asked while walking to the key hook in the kitchen to grab his keys and wallet.

I thought for a minute. My mind cleared and began to hyper-focus as the adrenaline pumped me into crisis mode. "It's in my studio in the loose block in the fireplace. I'll run get it if you'll start the car and bring it out front. Clarence, do you and Jo Ellen mind doing some errands for me while we're gone?"

"Of course. Whatever you need," Jo Ellen answered while Peter disappeared out the door.

"Okay. Jo Ellen, would you run into my bedroom and get the brown leather satchel in my closet? Inside should be a small, red address book and a passport. In the passport should be a list of names on a business card for an insurance company. If those things are still there, bring them and the whole bag to me," I said while walking toward the studio.

"Got it," she said and disappeared in the house.

"Follow me," I said to Clarence and broke into a run.

We opened my studio door and hurried over to a loose rock in the fireplace. I kept the key a secret from everyone except Peter. With the key, I had placed Jenny's note, some cash, and a piece of notebook paper.

"On this is a list of foods Jenny likes. We needed to make a grocery run anyway, so will you stock the kitchen? Also, will you call Mr. Thomas and find out what else needs to be done in the stables today? He'll get in touch with whoever can do it."

"I'll do it."

"Clarence, you need to spend time with--"

"Anni, trust me. I knew you when you lived there. That little girl and you were life rafts for each other. She kept you from swirling into a mourning depression, and you kept her safe from something. I never knew what, but the way you talked about it over dinner in New York after the race...I knew something was wrong."

"I didn't even know how wrong then. It got much worse Clarence--so much worse. I don't have time to explain, but depending on what the police say, she may stay with us. Do you think Jo Ellen would mind shopping for Jenny if we need clothes? I doubt she'll want to bring much."

"Oh she'll love it," Clarence's good eye held my face as seriously as possible.

"Okay. The cash should be enough for anything you need to buy. I've saved it, just in case," I choked back tears. My mind flashed to the day I received the key in the mail. All it said was "Just in case. Jenny." I sat down in the kitchen while Peter cooked dinner. I had stopped mid-sentence, so he looked at me. I had showed him the key and note, and he told me to keep it safe. He didn't laugh, thinking she was being a dramatic tween. That night we discussed exactly what we would do if we ever got a phone call like this. It was his idea to make sure we had cash set aside and hide everything like Jenny's father had told me to do about anything related to their family.

"The clock is ticking. Come on. Go find out what happened," Clarence bolstered me like he used to before a race when I fussed over Bronx and his safety.

I broke into a run the moment I stepped out of the studio. Peter had the car door open and engine running. Jo Ellen waved from the front porch. Whatever she yelled was lost in the door closing and the sound of speeding tires.

"I went ahead and called Bryan. He and his partner will meet us at the house. I told them that we have a key and she's scared. He said they wouldn't make it a big fanfare just in case, so no flashing lights or sirens, okay?"

"You called the police?" I said.

"Yes baby," he placed his hand on my wrist. I had been gripping the key. I loosened my hold and held his hand.

"Good. I don't know what we're walking into Peter. She said that 'they' are at the hospital. I can only imagine who that is by the way she was crying."

"What do we need to do next?"

"Get there as fast as we can, and we need to call her dad. She wouldn't be calling us if he wasn't on a mission."

"Okay," he nodded and pressed the gas more firmly.

Jo Ellen had placed the satchel in the floorboard. I bent to pick it up, opened it, and searched for the numbers and business card.

I dialed my phone. "Yes hello, my name is Annice Claire Wall Tatum, formerly MacKensie, and I was told to call Professor Green on Saturday if I needed to get in touch with Duncan Young about his daughter."

"I'm sorry Mrs. Tatum, but we are unable to get in touch with the professor at this time. Can you specify the urgency of this matter?"

"I am going to be arriving at his house in roughly ten to fifteen minutes and we are meeting the police who will assess the severity of the situation. His daughter got in touch with us and does not want to be in the custody of her mother or grandparents."

"I will see what I can do ma'am. Local or military police?"

"They live off base sir, so local."

My hands were shaking as we spoke. I had only tried contacting Jenny's dad once after her mother was rushed to the hospital. That was one of the longest seventy-two hours of my life, and I found out later that he didn't find out she almost died until he was debriefing back in Washington. When I hung up the phone, my mouth tasted metallic.

Peter squeezed my hand. "You thinking about when she lost the baby?"

I nodded and stared out the window, trying not to cry. Everything came flooding back to me.

Everything.

Memory Baggage
Anni

I was in the middle of a three-day shoot in a studio in New York that looked like someone threw up a Bali-wood version of Madonna's 1980s.

"Mrs. MacKensie, there's a call for you. They say it's urgent."

I waved my assistant off. I was desperately attempting to maintain my cool with this new model, "Dalphine" (pronounced "dahl-feen-ee"). I seriously believed that her real name was undoubtedly something she found boring since everything she did or I did caused her to yawn or sigh or roll her eyes. For the first time in my career, I was thirty seconds from firing a model on the spot. That was something my mentor did, not me.

"Mrs. MacKensie?"

With an unladylike grunt, I yelled in exasperation, "What! Unless it is life or death, I want to finish this shoot without the onset of a migraine, interruption, or this model!"

I spun around with my camera. My assistant Vickie cowered in her black trousers and boyfriend jacket. Behind me, the model was sputtering. I could feel everyone's eyes on me, but for once, I really didn't care. Then, I actually looked at my sweet assistant's face.

"Don't tell me it is life or death Vickie."

I didn't move. She didn't speak. I gripped my camera until my knuckles turned white. She was ashen. She was never ashen, not even on her elbows. My world faded to a phone. I watched it be placed in my hand and automatically shot it to my ear. I think Vickie took my camera. "Get that out of here, would you?" I cocked my head at "Dalphine" and straightened my shirt as though I was pressing a tie flat.

"Yes, hello?" I paused. "Yes, I am Annice." I paused irritably, "You know me Mr. Hobbes, I am the Mrs. Christopher MacKensie."

I remember seeing Keith and Stephen look at each other. Everyone knew that I never referred to myself in that manner. They tried to look as though they were monitoring the pictures on the terminals, but I knew they were peering at me because it was their hands that found me when my knees hit the floor. I don't remember arguing or how I got off the phone. I remember screaming over and over "No no no no no no no!"

Apparently my voice echoed down the halls. People came running. Vickie tried pushing them out of the studio. I was surrounded by arms and legs and fabric and a mixture of sweaty perfumes. I fought against whoever initially tried to hug me (Keith?) and started beating the floor with my phone. It shattered and cut my hands. Someone else's arms (Stephen's I think) wrapped around me and pulled me into an embrace while I wept.
In a blink, I arrived at the Nashville airport in clothes I can barely remember. I do remember wanting to peel everything off the moment I hit the Southern humidity. Nashville was a balmy 80

degrees Fahrenheit without a single cloud in sight. I hated Christopher for dying there.

A tall, slender man with a bulbous British nose held a card with my name typed on it. In my shock and grief, it had not dawned on me the family whom I married into and why a very formally dressed gentleman would be picking me up at the airport.

"Oh Jarvis!" I felt my lip quiver and chin shake.

"Hello mum," he said softly, with the height of decorum.

I stepped back and froze. I thought he was speaking to Christopher's mother. Then it dawned on me in a split second that she'd been dead over two years. I was now the sole MacKensie heir. Jarvis began taking my bags while I remained frozen. I grabbed his hand. He looked at me, and I noticed for the first time that his eyes were a striking blue with perfect crow's feet settled around them. The red rims of his eyes did not match the rest of his perfected demeanor. I squeezed his hand, and he squeezed mine in response.

We walked to the car in silence. When I saw it, my heart flew to my throat. Out of habit, I had expected to see Christopher's father's yellow 1957 Bentley Continental. It is the car we always used when we were in town. Christopher didn't know it, but I had arranged with Jarvis to have the Bentley moved to the new farm in New York once the Franklin estate was sold. Then, it dawned on me that the Bentley was what Christopher must have been driving since he rarely allowed Jarvis to drive him...

"Oh no Jarvis. I have to identify his body."

The MacKensies had very specific policies about body identification, embalming, and other details related to death. One particular rule was the closest relative (particularly spouse or the eldest child of the deceased) must identify a body with the family lawyer present in the event of a murder, suicide, or other untimely death where witnesses from the family are not present. We drove from the airport straight to the morgue where we met Mr. Hobbes and I had to identify Christopher's remains.

The head coroner escorted us to view the body through a glass window in a sterile gray hallway. His assistant pushed a rolling table with a white sheet in front of the window. He asked if I was ready. I nodded and grabbed Jarvis' hand. The assistant pulled the sheet down to reveal only Christopher's head, neck, and tops of his shoulders.

His face was so peaceful, but I knew how he died. I knew what was missing under the sheet. I knew about the drunk driver who clipped an eighteen-wheeler that fell onto Christopher's car. I knew that it wasn't instant. Mr. Hobbes had briefed me at some point prior to arriving in Nashville. He had affirmed that it was Christopher for the police department so that I could be contacted, but to be official and release the body to the funeral home for preparations, I had to be there.

Within seconds, Jarvis wrapped me in his arms as I wept seeing Christopher's sleepy seeming face. Mr. Hobbes told me later that Jarvis' face had gone white, but that sweet man never said a word. All the men waited in silence for me to acknowledge that it really was Christopher.

"It's him, but please sir. Do you know if he died alone?" I found myself asking the coroner.

The coroner looked old enough to be my grandfather. His dark, almost black eyes softened at my question. He said very softly that he was told an off-duty firefighter called "Big Jim" watched the accident happen, raced to the scene, and held Christopher in his arms as best he could while Christopher struggled to breathe and say "I love" over and over but never finishing his sentence.

I nodded while crying more and looked at Jarvis, "We need to find him so that I can thank him."

Jarvis nodded. Neither of us could speak. Mr. Hobbes wiped his eyes and muttered what we were all thinking, "It's so hard to believe it's really him, but there he is."

The assistant wheeled Christopher's body away from the window. Jarvis handed me his handkerchief. I wiped the remainder of my make-up, snot, and tears on it before clutching it and his hand for dear life.

Silently, we seemed to float from the coroner's office to the car. Mr. Hobbes handed me a folder and said, "I know you know Christopher's wishes, but here are those as outlined in his will for the funeral. The first page is a list of what you will need to do. I have marked off the arrangements I have already made, but you will need to accomplish the rest. I have included some event planners if it would help you to delegate as well as the family funeral home director's personal number."

I nodded mutely and received the manila folder. In his hands, it looked weightless. I may as well have accepted carrying a granite tombstone from the weight it seemed to be in my hands. I began to cry again and slipped into the car where Jarvis held the door open.

As the bends and hills of Nashville to Franklin passed my windows, I stared at the folder in my lap. Inside were details of a funeral I imagined our children planning when I was gray and wrinkled as opposed to being a childless photographer in my twenties. The weight of the folder leaped onto my chest. I curled up in the back seat and cried as though I heard the news of Christopher's death for the first time all over again.

All at once the car stopped. I heard Jarvis say something, but it didn't register in my mind as actual words. Decorum would have dictated that he wait in the front seat until I was composed and then he open my door. All I know is that Jarvis chose to ensure life over decorum when he appeared in the backseat with a paper bag and steady hand. I realized the bag smelled like French fries and fried chicken when I finally felt the sobs subside. I looked up at Jarvis with mascara streaks and while holding the bag at him, I laughed, "Now you've made me hungry."

"It's time," he responded softly.

I felt a vice grip squeeze all the air out of my lungs when I saw the house. "I don't know if I can go in there yet Jarvis."

He nodded as his own eyes brimmed with tears.

"I'll start making appointments. Let's not stay here yet," I looked at the manila folder and took a deep breath.

"Are you sure? No one is going to rush you to make funeral arrangements. You only arrived a short time ago."

I looked up into those fatherly eyes and smiled an almost frown, "I would rather get started than embrace life as yet another MacKensie widow."

He nodded again, patted my back, and went to the driver's seat. As he headed toward the funeral home, I called an event planner, my mother, and the funeral director. Thanks to Mr. Hobbes, everyone was positioned and ready to immediately be at my beckon call to make arrangements.

My mother quietly held my hand through every meeting and offered assistance in details when she saw a hole in the plan. Jarvis stood close at hand through everything. I barely remember the meetings, choosing the casket, and outlining the service. I ached through every meeting and put on my business face in an attempt to hold it together with people watching. To say "it was miserable" would be an understatement.

The flurry of details paled in comparison to the Southern tradition of casseroles and food shoved in front of me as comfort. The obituary had not even hit the newspaper when people and food showed up at our door. I became all too aware that most of my childhood friends still lived in Nashville with their high school sweethearts and/or bounty of children. Then Christopher's college friends from Vanderbilt and all of our parents' friends and acquaintances were showing up with casseroles and condolences. After the fifth poppy seed chicken casserole arrived, I looked at Jarvis and said, "It's official. I'm not in Manhattan anymore."

As the week spun like a tornado, I barely felt my feet under me as we drove to the funeral. My parents rode with Jarvis and I. We arrived extra early to meet with the funeral director and event planner. Together, they had orchestrated a funeral appropriate for a head of state. In my heart, I knew this funeral was for the people. The graveside service would be for me and for my grief.

People began to enter early to view Christopher's body. I hovered quietly out of sight so that people could have their moments alone. I couldn't bear the thought of standing by his casket all morning. Christopher's mother had done that when his father died. She was the stately wife in her perfect black chiffon dress, black gloves, and hat with a veil. Even though it was Christopher's funeral, I could see her in my mind's eye standing by his casket and evaluating each person arriving to mourn. I imagined her quietly approving each person, their grief, and their condolence. As this vision slipped from view, I recognized someone I didn't know even heard about the funeral.

All at once I knew Mr. Hobbes and Jarvis had worked to ensure that "Big Jim" was found. He literally towered over everyone in the room at six foot seven inches tall. I had never seen him in my life, but his crew cut and cleft in his chin had been perfectly described by an on-scene officer. I made my way through the throngs of people while calling "Big Jim" and trying to wave. When he saw me, he was able to part the crowd easily. I looked up at this giant of a hero and tears ran down my face. I lost all my words. His mouth contorted, and his cheeks turned red. We embraced like long lost family.

Wisely, Jarvis appeared by my side and guided us to the room that the pallbearers would take the casket before loading it into the hearse after the funeral. While the mourners lined up in the church sanctuary to view Christopher one last time, I asked Big Jim to tell me the story. He choked up immediately.

"I watched it all happen because I had noticed Brother's car. That yellow Bentley was a sight to behold. I was weaving through traffic to try to see what year and model when it happened," he stopped and pulled out his handkerchief. "I could hear the metal and see…" he shook his head. Jarvis silently brought us chairs. I glanced at him and mouthed, "Thank you." He nodded, but sweet Jarvis' chin trembled.

"Please. Only share what you are comfortable with," I found myself saying so calmly.

He nodded. "Cars went everywhere. I've never heard a sound like that scraping of metal on concrete. I was able to get my truck off the road and that's when I saw it. See, as a firefighter, we're trained to see what others might miss, and I could see Brother," he choked up again. "I raced to him to see what I could do. I won't tell you what it all looked like. How he looks in the casket…that's a better memory," he wiped his eyes. "Anyway, I wanted to help but when I got there Brother was…he was…" he choked again. "Ma'am, let's just say I knew he wasn't going to make it. I've seen some bad burns and people in a bad way, but car accidents are not something that I'm used to seeing quite like this, so I did what I knew to do. I held him. He was reaching out to me and saying something. As I leaned closer, I kept telling him that he was safe and this would all be over soon. Brother just nodded and kept saying 'I love' but couldn't finish the sentence."

That was when this massive man couldn't hold it together anymore. I didn't either. Somewhere as we embraced and cried, he said, "I don't even know his name. I just kept calling him Brother because that's what came out."

I looked him in the eyes and said, "His name is Christopher MacKensie."

Big Jim began to cry even harder. When he caught a breath he said, "There really are no accidents. See, my brother's name is Christopher and he's who I kept thinking of the whole time I held your husband. He always held me when I was little and had bad dreams. I kept praying that Brother would just feel like he was in a bad dream with no pain." Then he paused and straightened himself a bit and said, "Ma'am, may I hug you proper and tell you I love you? I feel that it was your husband's dying wish for you to know that he loved you."

I nodded and wept even harder. He held me as sobs wracked my body. Eventually as they subsided, I said, "Oh Big Jim. Now this is all my bad dream."

We embraced and wept again until a piano began to play. Jarvis ushered Big Jim to the sanctuary pews while I went to the back for the family processional. I saw the funeral director quietly telling all the mourners individually in line that the funeral needed to begin shortly. I avoided all eye contact. Christopher's relatives descended upon me the moment I appeared in the foyer. Their words and tears swirled around me while questioning who Big Jim was. I began to wonder when the last time I ate was before blinking and staring at Jarvis and my parents. The mourning line to the casket had finally dissipated, so event planner was lining up the relatives to enter while the pianist played church hymns.

I'm told the funeral was a gorgeous affair and the minister's eulogy was fitting. My father gave the obituary through tears and gold-wire reading glasses. I remember specifically asking Jarvis to sit on one side of me while I had my mother on the other. Jarvis was dressed in an Italian three-piece suit with a purple bow tie. I remember him wearing that exact ensemble to Christopher's mother's funeral. I never saw even the bow tie again after Christopher died.

I remember noticing that the pianist wore a tuxedo morning coat with a white bow tie and that the picture slide show sent up a ridiculous number of sobs from Christopher's relatives. While the funeral and drive to the graveside are a blur, the graveside service is as crystal clear as if it happened a minute ago.

I had requested that only family go to the graveside. I endured a painfully long receiving line before going to the cemetery, so when I arrived, I had forgotten everything I was supposed to say.

There were only chairs for 20, but at least 50 people spilled from beneath the tent in standing room only. I knew this was the relatives' doing, but I said nothing. The minister at the funeral was actually the same dear man who married Christopher and I. It took a few moments for Pastor Mark to quiet everyone to begin the graveside service. The pastor was rather hoarse from crying, so his voice was barely audible over the crowd.

"Most of you are family and remember me from Anni and Christopher's wedding. I never imagined I would be doing Chris' funeral because we actually joked that he needed to speak at mine," Mark smiled but paused as his mouth frowned and jaw quivered. "But ol' Chris and I agreed that Anni was the best one to speak at either of ours."

An audible gasp erupted across the tent. I smoothed the skirt of my black lace dress and stood. Jarvis stood to my right, slightly out of the line of vision. He handed me a small bible with my forgotten notes. I blushed before turning to look at the surrounding people straight in the eye. Every pair that I could see, I looked right into them. For approximately half a minute total I sought and held the gaze of each mourner. Then quietly I said, "None of you should be here."

Everyone shifted uncomfortably and averted their eyes to the fake grass tarp that the funeral home had placed on the ground to protect the graves we were unfortunately positioned over for our funeral. I could see my mother white-knuckle her handkerchief and her nose flush red again with tears.

I cleared my throat again, "None of you should be here because Christopher shouldn't have died. He should have never been in Nashville because we should have wrapped things up with selling the farm a year ago."

His relatives gasped and looked at one another. I could see dollar signs winking and blinking above their heads, like they dodged a bullet. I saw one of his aunts mouth to the other, "I'm glad that didn't go through."

I felt my insides turn to iron, and my heart burned in my throat. I looked at my notes. Mixed with the blue cardstock was a picture I still keep in that Bible. Out of nowhere, I began to tell the story from the photograph, "One day when we were still courting, Christopher showed up at a nightmare of a photo-shoot in the dead of winter in Central Park. He held a disposable cup of coffee from my favorite barista at Third Rail Coffee. 'I brought everyone some pastries too. Your models look like they need to eat something,' he had whispered to me," I laughed again like it had just happened and continued, "His appearance reenergized the shoot, and the best shots of the day happened after those skinny models got some carbs. (God bless Southern boys). While my assistants shut everything down and shooed me away, Christopher and I slipped over to the ice skating rink. That man pulled on rented ice skates while placing his Italian leather loafers on the edge of the rink. Without a thought, he began to show off and skate backward in his three-piece suit under a Burberry trench coat. With legs as shaky as a newborn deer, I placed my skates on the ice and prayed I wouldn't wipe out in front of this perfectly put together man who was courting me. And that's what this traditionally modern man called it, 'Courting.' As he grabbed my hands to help me skate, he said while laughing at me, 'I love courting you Annice.' He's the only person besides my parents that actually calls me Annice," I paused to swallow a rising tear in my throat. "Anyway, as terrible as a skater as I was, I'm still a fabulous photographer. Eventually I got him to leave me by the side and I pulled my camera out of my purse. He began to skate and spin in the middle of the ice. Arms outstretched, tongue hanging out because snow was starting to fall. This is the picture I snapped."

I held up the picture. His tall figure was a swath of black against the bright white snow and ice under evening lights. In the instant prior, he had stopped sticking his tongue out to the sky and looked at me, arms still outstretched and skating toward me. His mouth open in a laugh and cheeks bright red with cold.

Quietly, so very quietly, I said, "This man, so full of life, grabbed every moment with this kind of abandon, and he invited me into that world of living life to the fullest. It was never about him. Life was about love and passion and destiny and finding your calling and generosity and hope and sharing the Good News with every person you meet. This is the man whose body lies mutilated in this casket, but this man in this picture--this is memory we will carry. This is the life that touched us. This is the brilliant flame that could not be extinguished and made his mark on the world in an effort to change it."

I looked at his casket, piled with flowers, and said, "I pray I do your legacy justice and that I too change the world for the better. Thank you for teaching me that I matter as more than my job or role in life but I matter as a person who is living and breathing with a face and a name and a destiny. Thank you for showing me how God is present in the everyday, not just the big ways."

Tears rolled down my face as I tried and failed to read my notes.

Finally, I said, "The body we are interring in the ground is not Christopher. Remember that. This is just the vessel. He is gone to be with The Lord he served with all his heart and with full abandon and joy. He endures no pain, no anguish, and no agony any more. He is set free. We are who mourn the spark and ember of his life, removed from us, but if you stand here with no certainty of where you will go, look at the life and legacy of this man of God. He knew where he was going, and for that, I am grateful. His certainty comforts my grief because I know I will join him one day. If you have no certainty, now is your chance to receive salvation. Now is your chance to turn and claim Jesus is your savior. For you to choose to live a life for the Lord would make Christopher's death, not in vain or a terrible tragedy. It would be an ever-fixed mark as a seed planted to spark your eternity in Heaven. Don't miss your opportunity."

I took a deep breath and continued while staring at his casket, "While you are gone dear heart of mine, I mourn. I mourn the loss of you, the smell of you, the laughter of you. Oh dear heart of mine, I miss you so much. Until one day in the future my love, until one day."

Softly the tears spilled down my cheeks and covered my chest and hands. I looked at Pastor Mark and nodded for him to close out the service and pray.

I could see the surprise on his face that I had given a salvation call at a funeral. It wasn't in my notes. It literally spilled out of my heart because on the back of the photograph Christopher had written, "I don't want just one day with you; I want an eternity with God and you that are filled with moments like this one."

He had secretly snagged that digital image from computer, had it printed, and slipped it into that small Bible he gave me as an engagement gift. After the funeral, it was weeks before I could even open my Bible again.

The estate house was filled with people for the wake by the time Jarvis, my parents, and I arrived after the graveside service. We were the last to leave because we waited for the gravediggers to cover Christopher's casket with dirt. Softly my father said, "It's done Annice."

His funeral was done, but the grief wasn't. I remember walking from room to room as people shared memories of Christopher, his family, and chatted about the estate when they thought I was out of earshot. I thanked people for coming and celebrating Christopher's life. I seemed to move underwater, as though floating in dream.

Sometimes words would register and faces would make sense. Other moments I felt and remembered nothing of walking from place to place. Eventually, my parents, Mr. Hobbes, and Jarvis herded people out of the house.

For the first time since my arrival in Nashville, I actually slept at the estate house. It was far too late to go to my parents' house or stay in a hotel. I curled up in Christopher's bed that night and didn't move for days, possibly weeks. My pajamas began to stink. My hair was a mess. I allowed my cell phone to die so that I wouldn't have to answer phone calls. I lost track of time. I know I ate because Jarvis and occasionally my mother would show up to bring me food.

I vaguely remember my mother convincing me to change pajamas once. I might have showered. Mostly, I would go through pictures, emails, and listen to his voicemail message while weeping. During the day, I cried for the loss of our plans: the racing horses, the farm in upstate New York, our children dressed by designers and raised on runways and horses, the non-profit he wanted to start to help rehabilitate homeless girls in New York, and even the little things like the vacations we'd dreamed and tables we considered buying. I couldn't read the condolences on my email or blog or even letters in the mail. I swirled into a pile of paper, bedclothes, and tears.

At night, I would wake up from nightmares of all varying degrees of grotesque or upsetting as I relived my imaginations' concoction of Christopher's last moments, saw his body, and a number of other iterations. I went through a period of insomnia and prescription sleep aids. I don't recall how the medication got placed in my hands, but it did. I think I found it in the master bathroom medicine cabinet. The cabinet was brimming with all sorts of supplements and prescriptions.

Honestly, a therapist could have come to the house and evaluated me. I have no memory of it. What I remember most clearly is holding Christopher's teddy bear and crying.

Pills didn't really solve anything.

I was still alone. I was so alone that I began to see Loneliness and Grief standing like real-life jailers outside my room and leading my path everywhere I went. They were cloaked in heavy wool trench coats and wore thick leather gun belts over their coats. They reminded me of shadowed versions of the Russian military men we met during a Siberian photo shoot.

The emblem on their shoulders was of black lion-like creatures with "fear" written above the animal. One night I actually saw the chains around my wrists and ankles and waist.

As I noticed these horrible chains, a light cut through my consciousness. Whether I was awake or dreaming didn't matter. I began to realize how long it had been since I picked up my camera or even answered my phone. My ears had been deaf to the calls, emails, and voicemails. I had ignored condolence letters and flowers and barely functioned when Jarvis would ask me to tea every afternoon.

Suddenly, I looked to my jailers, Loneliness and Grief, at my door. They stood with fear, guilt, shame, and an army of minions extending down the hallway. Loneliness and Grief took off their cloaks to reveal the shiniest of suits. They suddenly seemed more warm and more accessible. They entered the room and revealed to be carrying the weighted metal balls at the end of my chains.

Loneliness said in a voice that echoed through my soul, "But are those calls and emails and letters even real? No one has shown up. No one has flown down to hold you as you have cried yourself to sleep. We have been here to hold you and help you through this."

Grief chimed in with a hollow yet honeyed voice, "And we actually know what you have been through because we have been with you. I have been with you the longest through this. I am who held your hand. Don't you want me to keep working with you in your time of need?"

As I started to speak, my vision shifted as though I was watching a movie. I saw Grief begin as a seed of emotion that I planted and watered. When the time came to harvest it and to burn it like incense to release it, I instead brought it into my house where it grew into a Presence. What was once a good thing had become an encroaching, prowling beast in my environment. Then I looked at Loneliness and saw how it had started as a baggage tag on my identity suitcase of Widow. I had placed the suitcase next to my Grief plant, and as Grief grew, it had started talking to Loneliness, which started growing in its own right. The tag grew to the size of the Widow baggage. Then, it began to grow feet and turn into its own, scaled form.

Gone were the shadows in designer suits that seemed to be lifting the burdens of my weight of my circumstance and new identity. My throat felt seized by hands, and suddenly, I saw the lion-like creature from the emblems on their arms. It appeared to be in gray-scale and void of actual color or true life as it bounded down the hallway toward me and leaped onto me, which removed Loneliness and Grief for a moment. It had the stench of rotting meat on its breath. The hands around my neck were like paws of massive proportions. Fear spoke.

Its voice rumbled like a washing machine you mistake for the clap of thunder, but you jump in surprise because you aren't expecting a noise across your house.

It said, "You can't survive without them, and you need me to run your life. This is who you are. You are a widow, grief-stricken, nothing else. No one will want to marry you for love any more. They will only see your money. They will only see that you are a young widow who couldn't keep her first husband alive. You are nothing. You are worthless, so just let us run your life. If you let me be the general of your army, I will dispatch Control to you, and you will wield it with such power that you will rise even higher in authority as a photographer and presence in the fashion industry. Trust me. You want Control to be your lieutenant."

The shock of Fear smothering my throat and my voice absolutely shook my person. I couldn't speak. I lay in my bed wondering what crazy pills I had taken and had the thought, "Well if I pray, maybe this will be over...Jesus, I'm scared. I don't want this. Help. I know you know me and you saved me, so what's happening? Help!"

The voice that cut through the room echoed like real thunder, but louder. Lightning cracked and a hollow howl similar to a pack of wolves echoed through my house. Love entered my room so tangibly that my room was flooded with a thick red cloud that smelled like lilies and incense and chocolate chip cookies.

If it was just a dream, it was more real than life. When Love entered, His face was calm and He held my hands. The chains fell with the most resounding thud. I felt lighter, more alive. I wanted to speak, to ask a million questions, but He wrapped a blanket of peace around me like a robe. I felt so small and insignificant as He tended to me like a mother to a sick child. Tears rolled down my cheeks. He smiled and collected each one into a crystal vial that He slipped back into His pocket as He sat next to me. He grabbed my hands and said in a voice that cut through my entire person, "Soon." I think I nodded because He smiled, squeezed my hands, and left.

The cloud lingered for hours, and I felt the blanket of peace around me for days even though its physical appearance disappeared with the red cloud.

The next morning, Jarvis came into the room, turned on the shower, and threw back the curtains. I muttered and tried to hide under the covers. He threw back the covers, picked me up, and placed me in the shower in my clothes. I sputtered and squealed.

"You smell like a farm animal. I'm stripping your bed. If you need a steel wool pad to get through your grime, let me know. I expect you downstairs for high tea in an hour," he yelled over the rush of the shower water.

I turned the showerhead to the wall so I could get out of my sopping wet pajamas. I tossed them out of the shower before obediently scrubbing the "grime" out of my hair and off my person. When I stepped out of the shower with my skin turned pink by the heat, I saw that Jarvis had indeed stripped the bed, removed my wet pajamas, and placed my suitcase open on the sink counter.

When I appeared for our first tea, I wore yoga pants that had never been in a yoga studio and a tunic t-shirt and slippers. Timidly, I sat and received the cup of tea he placed in my hands.

"Don't forget to eat," he said before disappearing back into the kitchen.

I never found out what prompted him to do this, but thank God for the British and their tea. He informed me as we finished tea that I could "take my reprieve in the master bedroom because I need to quarantine your room from the stench and possible infestation."

Humbly I nodded and thanked him for tea. My voice came out in a hoarse whisper. The next day he threw back the curtains again in time for tea. I quickly volunteered to shower and dress so as to avoid another pajama-clad dump. On the third morning, I managed to get up and make myself cereal before asking Jarvis for stationary to write 'Thank You' notes for the flowers, donations, and attendance to the funeral. I stopped weeping through my correspondences long enough to take tea. By the fourth day, it became a ritual that no matter what we were doing, we would stop for tea and sit together as friends. I began to pivot my day by teatime in an effort to find some semblance of normalcy.

Eventually, Mr. Hobbes showed up unannounced thanks to my dead cell phone. Apparently he had been trying to reach me to discuss the reading of the will and how to handle the MacKensie estate. He had cousins and aunts breathing down his neck. They were all vying for certain paintings and pieces of furniture.

"I'm just glad to know you are alive. It's been almost ten days since the funeral and no one has heard from you," he said as he put on his hat before leaving with a promise to return for tea the next day.

When I charged my phone, I realized the relatives had been attempting to reach me, which is why they had turned their focus onto Mr. Hobbes. I had two voice mails from my mother offering options of where to live while I sold off the estate. Everyone assumed I wanted my life back in New York. They assumed that my career as a fashion photographer was everything I wanted to return to because it was my normal. Without Christopher, nothing was normal.

As I relayed the voicemails to Mr. Hobbes and Jarvis over tea, I noted that the relatives didn't dare ask for horses or land or even the house. They wanted to know what I was doing with "sentimental items" like the Ming vase, "the dancer painting" (a Degas), the Louis XVI marble topped sideboard, and a Pollack sketch. Mr. Hobbes sipped his tea and rolled his eyes.

"Honestly, after your graveside speech, I'm surprised they had the gall to ask after anything," he huffed through his Wyatt Earp style mustache. "I guess they are certain where they are going and are fine with fire."

I choked on my tea. "Mr. Hobbes!"

"If they wanted a sentimental item, they would ask for the hand-crocheted lace their grandmother made or pewter family pitcher that dates back to the colonies," Jarvis sputtered as he poured me another cup of Earl Grey.

Regaining my composure as I dropped brown sugar cubes into my Earl Grey, I smiled, "I love that lace. Did you know Mrs. MacKensie actually let me use some of the pieces as inspiration for my bridal gown? My designer used some ladies in Italy to custom make the lace because Christopher had told me to spare no expense to get the lace just right. Mama was relieved Christopher bought the dress for me because it cost almost half the wedding budget she and Dad had set aside."

"I remember. You missed the discussion here of the cost of the dress," Jarvis settled next to me with his cup of tea.

"Oh no! Jarvis! What happened?"

"Oh you know it isn't my place."

"Jarvis, we are passed decorum. Dish," I tucked my feet under me in my chair and leaned forward eagerly.

He looked around as though Mrs. MacKensie might rise from the dead two years later. Knowing her, she might just to spite us. Smiling mischievously, Jarvis launched into how she started throwing the flowers she was arranging at Christopher across the foyer. We sipped tea and began to forget what brought us together in this house in this season. Mr. Hobbes joined in with stories of Mrs. MacKensie's tirades in his office that had become quite the talk of the high society. Eventually the teapot emptied but our laughter didn't. Jarvis started more water. Mr. Hobbes and I then launched into discussing a formal reading of the will.

A horribly traditional act, I knew the reading had to be done. Since the relatives had been calling him daily, Mr. Hobbes said he would deftly slip into conversation when he was arriving to read the will in two days time. "As long as they are not invited. This is supposed to be private with just you, me, and Jarvis," I said with a smirk as Jarvis reentered with fresh tea.

"Don't worry. I'll make sure to mention you want it to be private," Mr. Hobbes winked and took another homemade scone. "Just get prepared."

In preparation of the reading of the will, I actually didn't anticipate any of the relatives showing up, but Jarvis assured me that I should dress for tea that day.

Like clockwork, Mr. Hobbes and a gaggle of unannounced relatives appeared for the reading of the will. Everyone settled in the formal dining room. (Earlier that morning, Jarvis hid the silver and china out in the old kitchen in boxes labeled "Everyday Linens.") As if to make a point, I noticed that Jarvis had placed the family pewter pitcher on the table next to a fifteen-dollar glass one with water and glasses. Unsurprisingly, he had anticipated the unannounced relatives.

Mr. Hobbes and I entered the dining room last. He was fumbling with his hat while sweating through an ill-fitting tweed suit. I patted his shoulder, "Mr. Hobbes, it will be okay."

"I know darlin' but Matilda," he lowered his voice to hardly above a whisper, "spanked me as we walked in the door! That woman could be my daughter!"

I tried not to laugh. Matilda had recently lost her third husband to a heart attack. She also knew that Mr. Hobbes was paid well enough during Mrs. MacKensie's lifetime that he really didn't have to ever keep any of his other clients.

"Take that as a compliment. You are a striking old bachelor," I smiled and adjusted his plaid bow tie while everyone else entered the dining room under Jarvis' direction.

He smiled and stood straighter after I pressed his tie flat, but he continued to whisper out of earshot of the relatives, "Thank you dear. Now listen, I've been thinking about your mother's voice mails about where to live. You really should consider Seymour's daughter's offer to live in their guesthouse while you sell the estate and parcel out various items. Seymour and his wife were dear friends of Mrs. MacKensie's, so I know his daughter will treat you well. Besides, being in Tennessee while you settle matters will be much simpler than dealing with it all from Manhattan."

"I am considering it. I don't know if I can live with the ghosts of several generations of 'Mrs. MacKensies' haunting me or other special living ones," I nodded my head toward the table.

He smirked and covered his face with his leather portfolio. Jarvis remained standing by the door in his suit. I sat near Mr. Hobbes at an angle that allowed me to watch the relatives out of the corner of my eye. After the initial specifications that in the event of his death, Christopher left literally everything to me and entrusted me to keep, sell, or gift any item of my choosing "save this one small detail." Mr. Hobbes paused dramatically. (I tend to believe he did that for my benefit). The relatives leaned in like the black wearing vultures that they were.

"I leave my mother's city house, his choice of bed and table linens, the silver candelabras, the Louis XVI marble topped sideboard, and his choice of any two paintings from either Tennessee home to our beloved butler and family friend, Clive Jarvis, Jr. I also leave him the money to cover his pension in the amount of--"

The audible gasps and murmurs from the family drowned the very high figure Christopher had left Jarvis. If any of them had been listening, I think both aunts might have had strokes. I hurried to Jarvis' side. He had paled and begun to sweat. I urged him to sit, trying not to laugh at the flustered cousins who were now beginning to stand outraged and threatening to contest the will.

Christopher had covered that with Mr. Hobbes' next line of "And should any of my relatives be at the reading of this will despite not being invited, Mr. Hobbes should take note of their names and instruct my wife not to parcel out any of the family heirlooms to those present, most particularly the art, horses, and furniture."

There was very little recovery from this announcement. I ignored everyone except Jarvis, who had tears running down his face. I heard sputtering and chairs clattering and scooting away from the table.

"Why didn't you tell me?" he finally managed after blowing his nose into his handkerchief.

I smiled and shrugged. "And miss this? Are you kidding?"

He chuckled with me. I helped him to his feet as the relatives hurried out the door. Dutifully, Mr. Hobbes took note of each relative that was there.

As soon as they all left, we all three laughed and laughed as though a balloon had finally burst. In the following days, Jarvis and I continued to mourn and laugh together until I fitfully arranged the house for a realtor as well as helped him go through all the furnishings in the downtown Franklin "city house."

My high school friend Clara helped us put his whole decorating scheme together and decide what pieces worked best to keep versus sell. Somehow, I had been convinced to sell quite a bit of furniture and art via auction, so Jarvis and I were both in a time crunch to identify the entire lot for the auction house.

When both houses seemed fitfully situated, I made the long trip back to Manhattan to go through our city life, alone. Jarvis offered to come with me. I asked if he would give me a few days to build up some pajama stench first. He laughed.

In the city that never sleeps, I worked non-stop. My time off was felt at the magazine, but timidly, everyone offered condolences and attempted to walk around me on tiptoe. I had been gone approximately forty-five days.

I overheard two interns talking in the break room that they had heard my lawyer had called the Editor-in-Chief of our parent company magazine and as well as the Editor-in-Chief of *Best Dressed*. According to the interns, Mr. Hobbes had personally called to handle my transition after the funeral. My mouth went dry. I realized I must have been in horrible shape if Mr. Hobbes had realized I would need more than the initial 30 days I put in before racing to Nashville. To make matters worse, even the interns were talking about me.

As the senior photography editor, this wasn't unusual, but people didn't actually know my personal life. I had an inkling it was speculated upon, but most people didn't mess with me (especially underlings). If you were in the industry, you knew how I started at 17 and worked relentlessly under one of the most demanding international fashion photographers that *did not* accept apprentices. *He accepted me.* That acceptance itself spoke volumes of my work ethic and talent, but these two interns in their designer shoes and super tight skirts were talking about my husband's funeral and how I was coping.

"Coping" now topped the list of worst words in the English language for me. My throat started to close, and my palms grew sweaty. I hurriedly aimed for a bathroom to heave out my embarrassment and last bits of pride.

Instead, I bumped into the arms of Kevin, *Best Dressed*'s Editor-in-Chief. My face changed three shades of red and maybe a few shades of green.

"Hey, it's great to have you back. I know we haven't gotten to have our official meeting to catch you up, but I hope staff meeting helped this morning?" he said gently.

Nothing about Kevin was ever gentle. A temper that could raise Cain was only matched by the ruthless way he critiqued everything with perfectionism. I was startled to see his bright blue eyes slightly red and teary.

"Thanks Kevin. It did. Everyone in photography really kept the ball rolling. I'm not behind on anything," I managed to say. "Are you okay?"

His nose turned red, and he smiled weakly. "Of course. Never better. I'll see you in my office in fifteen?"

He hurried away without waiting for an answer. It turned out that his uncle who was like a father to him had also died in a car accident the year prior. He shared with me openly about it in our meeting and said very kindly, "So I can't imagine your grief.

If you need more time off, no one will begrudge you."

Best Dressed began its life as an online fashion magazine to pioneer the Wild West World of the Internet. The idea was to create a space for more fluidity and artistry within the industry. Print standards and advertisements were much more lenient, so as photography editor, I actually worked on text content and formatting as well as the photography.

Through my leadership and photography, the magazine was flourishing. I could post from anywhere I had an Internet connection, and I used that information to my advantage with Kevin.

"Look. I'm not going to mince words with you Kevin. You love this job. You are great at spearheading this project. In two years we have advanced sales for the parent magazine as well as bolstered an international following that has rejuvenated the high fashion industry among laypeople. What we are doing is incredible, and I don't want your job," I watched him shift his weight in his seat. His eyes betrayed the poker face. He was relieved.

I continued, "With the big launch of this live tweet thing during every fashion week, real time updates on the website during all the parties and from the different runways, and the follow up articles, we are going to be in war room mode constantly. How about I continue to run things for my department remotely when I have to be in Tennessee as I am settling the estate? Then you can continue to build the brand knowing that this department won't have a lull."

Freelancing was not a new concept, but working remotely, especially as an editor, was a new concept for the magazine. Little did we know that this would help keep *Best Dressed* from being an expendable asset.

Basically, the housing market was showing hiccups already, but people were snatching real estate quickly. Somehow despite my fragile state of mind to get to Nashville to plan Christopher's funeral, I had managed to call our realtor that secured the farmhouse. Despite shocking the poor man with Christopher's death, I had informed him that we would need to move immediately on selling the farm and the flat in Manhattan. He tried to convince me not to make any rash decisions, but apparently (I have no memory of this), I said to him, "Honey. We snatched that farmhouse and practically flipped it in 30 days and I have no attachment to that place minus a hope and a dream with a man who is now dead. Do I need to spell it out for you on how this pays you twice as well as selling the apartment? I will need a little more time on the flat so don't list it until after the funeral, but they are both selling. Period. I know myself."

He was compliant and had his assistant meet me at the airport with all the paperwork I would need to sign. The farm had a buyer before the funeral with an offer for twice what we paid because they wanted to keep most of the horses.

The flat had a buyer within a week of being on the market. My mentor still had his studio in the city but was living most of the time in Paris. He offered for me to stay at his place while I sorted through everything.

To manage things in Nashville, I chose to take Seymour's daughter's offer to stay in the guesthouse. The guesthouse arrangement worked because all I had to do was be on call for emergencies when I was home. The rent was laughable, and they allowed me to arrange the house however I chose. The main appeal was not being stuck south of Franklin, TN in a gigantic antebellum house, alone, while a realtor attempted to sell the very lavish estate. Little did any of us realize that the housing hiccups were about to be a market implosion to kick off an economic recession.

Even though the housing market was declining, the rich were still purchasing estates. Many had chosen to transplant themselves from places like Manhattan and Malibu to lower cost-of-living areas such as Atlanta and Nashville. The tucked-away nature of a lavish estate in Franklin was "sure to draw celebrities and wealthy business people."

At least, that's what Cecily the realtor said. Very likable with a shock of Lucille Ball hair, I felt somewhat assured about my decision to stay in Seymour's daughter's guesthouse for 6 months.

"You'll have it sold by Christmas," Mr. Hobbes declared over lunch at his usual spot, Tin Angel.

"Thank you for your assurance Mr. Hobbes," I smiled hopefully between mouthfuls of étouffé.

He sipped his sweet tea and continued, "I mean, you have your life in New York darlin' and it took quite a bit for you to get established up there. I know how you'd just hate to leave that swirlin' fashion world."

I laughed and was fortunately saved by the reason we were even at this lunch meeting: donating art to the museum.

We were finalizing their procurement of some of my inherited art. Partially a blow to the relatives, I chose to donate to one of Mrs. MacKensie's favorite places. Much of the family collection could easily have been sold in New York or donated to the Tate, but I enjoyed the thought of the aunts and cousins walking through the local museum to see "their" art and not touch it. Malicious? Probably, but Christopher's death didn't exactly help me to see sunshine and rainbows, especially about his greedy relatives.

Unusually late, the director was towing one of her curators to join us for lunch. A quiet young man with dark brown curls, the curator fidgeted with his tie as we discussed business and they ordered lunch. Their late arrival kept me from discussing with Mr. Hobbes the truth of my New York situation.

"Mrs. MacKensie, I'd like to introduce you to Wendell. He will be handling..."

I smiled warmly and shook his hand with Southern, ladylike precision. I watched a look of surprise appear and disappear from his eyes. I smiled to myself and remembered Christopher's reaction to my handshake being in mock Southern drawl, "Well I declare. Of all the girls in the Big City, I fall in love with a mannered one. Don't tell me you're from Tennessee like me?"

"Wonderful. It's a pleasure to meet you."

"Likewise Mrs. MacKensie," he smiled and started to say something but the director cut him off.

Mr. Hobbes began launching into the tedious details of paperwork and authenticity. Bored, I began to think about how Jarvis and I enjoyed going through the estate. I was overwhelmed by the amount of art. Apparently, Christopher's family had been prolific collectors going back for literally centuries. I could open my own museum with the amount of paintings, sculptures, sketches, and photographs in the houses and storage. The family's passion for art only matched their passion for horses, but fortunately, the art did not necessarily revolve around that particular passion.

"What do you think Mrs. MacKensie?"

"Pardon?"

"The Gala auction?"

"Oh, sorry. I was thinking about how glad I am that the MacKensie family didn't tend to collect horse paintings or have their horses' portraits as their main art," I admitted.

Everyone chuckled as they do with a rich widow who is giving you something you want or who might. I began to wonder how Mrs. MacKensie handled it. She collected much of the family art and made a point to follow trends locally and internationally. This often caused her to attend auctions in New York or to send Jarvis and Mr. Hobbes to London. She found art to be almost an accessory as much as rotated pieces into each house according to the season and if they fit a party she was throwing. Often, she would change the art in a bedroom where she hosted an overnight guest to fit that person's specific taste. She was known to purchase a sculpture that specifically fit her theme for her annual black tie spring tea. Then, she would add it to the sculpture garden, sell it, or donate it. Her choice typically depended on her mood and the success of the tea.

The waitress interrupted to refill our drinks. Mr. Hobbes asked for the dessert menu, and the waitress smiled asking if he really wanted something besides his usual crème brûlée.

He laughed and said, "Sugar, you know that's what I want with a spot o' coffee, but Mrs. MacKensie might want a peek." I rolled my eyes at him. That man believed dessert solved all problems. Between he and Jarvis' teas and cakes, I was going to be the fat, rich widow before the year was up.

"I was asking if you'd be interested in attending the annual Gala. Your husband and his mother often frequented it, and we'd be most obliged if you'd attend. Also, with your donation, we'd love to honor you there as well," Alice proposed congenially.

"Thank you Alice, and please, remember to call me Anni. I keep looking for my mother-in-law when you say that," I laughed and waved at our waitress for more coffee. "I would be delighted to attend."

Wendell cleared his throat as though to make his existence known. We all stared at him. He blushed visibly and apologized. Dessert was served, so Mr. Hobbes took over discussing with Alice when he might meet with her again. Smooth as silk, he swept that woman into a date before she realized what had happened. Wendell, on the other hand, fumbled at making conversation with me.

"Okay Wendell," I patted his hand like an old mother, "you are either trying to ask me on a date or ask me for something, so why don't you get on with it?"

He blushed even deeper red before he stuttered: "I wouldn't... I mean..."

I crossed my arms and sat back. "Choose your words carefully. I believe we're the same age Wendell, so don't treat me like I'm one of the 80 year old widows you have dealt with in the past."

He swallowed, straightened, and finally spoke. "Actually, um, Anni, I am a big fan of your work, and I would love to curate a show involving fashion photography."

"Ah, I see. A retrospective? Current photography? Magazine covers? What were you thinking?"

The conversation moved to coffee with just Wendell and I discussing who we could bring in on the show. With my creative juices flowing, it was wonderful to race to the guesthouse where I had set up a makeshift studio and office. I began strategizing who I could call in favors to connect the show to NY while using it as a marketing tool for *Best Dressed*. Kevin loved the collaborative idea and suddenly he began wanting me to continue working remotely as much as possible.

"Your inspiration is unlike anything I've seen with you on location. The fall fashion week run is going to be inspiring, so hurry back and don't screw this up," Kevin warned.

As it turned out, being able to work remotely and not print our magazine worked well in our favor as a whole over the next year. The parent magazine company had to shut down other magazines in the family and lay off huge numbers as people dropped print advertising. *Best Dressed* soared as the free gem covering the high fashion industry, but things began to grow bleak for everyone around me. The pressure to stay at *Best Dressed* was growing less and less because I could see the writing on the wall.

While interns suddenly disappeared from circulation and editorial staff from the parent magazine began showing up more and more, staff meetings grew increasingly intense. When I wasn't in the office and "sat" in meetings via conference call, I could hear the anxiety in the voices of all the editors even in what they were pitching on a daily basis.

People were losing jobs--actual careers--around us and were unable to find something else, even waiting tables and retail jobs. Everyone sat on pins and needles, waiting for the other stiletto to drop.

For me, the Franklin house wasn't selling, but I wasn't bothered. Our CPA and banker were giving me updates almost daily about the state of my finances. Unbeknownst to me, Christopher's family had invested very wisely for years. While other people lost their retirement almost overnight, I had a vast majority of our money sitting practically untouched by the recession. It was particularly helpful that we did everything debt-free, so when the New York real estate sold, all that profit was cash in my pocket. The number was staggering. I was literally sitting in a financial situation people wished to happen upon them even during opulent seasons.

As the recession spiraled and people were attempting to think outside the box for job ideas, I often heard the question, "If money were no object, what would you do?"

The question hit my gut like a ton of bricks. All I could think about was that none of them posed how the money being no object would happen. I would receive my daily financial updates and feel sick at my stomach with no clue how to answer that same question for my own reality. Money was no object, yet I would have exchanged my life for a tent in Africa serving orphans if Christopher could be with me.

The actual stiletto high-heeled shoe I was waiting for to drop was about Seymour's daughter--Jenny's mother. Jenny had shown up on the guesthouse doorstep in with freckles, bare feet, and overalls. Her ribbons were falling out of her braids. "You know how my mom is pregnant?"

"Well hi Jenny. Yes…"

"Something is wrong."

Without thinking I grabbed my purse and Jenny's hand and broke into a run. You must understand that at first, the arrangement to move into the guesthouse happened because they had the empty space and wanted to collect some rent.

Jenny's mother was put on bed rest immediately following her surprise diagnosis of pregnancy at thirty-seven. A lithe and athletic creature, she spent more time on her feet in the comfort of her own home than in bed. She reached 22 weeks in her pregnancy shortly after I moved in and Jenny showed up at my door with her "Something is wrong" statement.

When we raced together in the house, Jenny's mother was sitting in the living room floor holding her temples and crying. "She needs to go to the doctor because her head hurts and she isn't seeing right," Jenny had told me as we fled from the guesthouse.

Jenny and I walked her mother between us to the car and raced her to the emergency room where she was diagnosed with early-onset preeclampsia. She stayed in the hospital until her blood pressure and kidneys seemed to stabilize. She then was released to non-hospitalized bed rest for the rest of the pregnancy. She had to be wheeled in a wheelchair to move more than a few feet.

Jenny's grandparents (Seymour and his wife) moved into the main house. I stayed in the main house every two weeks while they handled personal business at their farm. This made the guesthouse arrangement became one of necessary help.

Any minute I expected to call an ambulance and Jenny's father. Duncan had been on back-to-back cases for military intelligence, so I barely knew his face aside from the pictures in the house. I was given a strict protocol on who to contact, when, and how to speak to them should an emergency arise.

The face I knew best was little Jenny's. While her mother was stuck in the bed and her grandparents taking over the house, Jenny would appear on my doorstep. "I wanted to know what you were doing," she'd say timidly, staring at my welcome mat.

Typically I would show her my latest projects and explain to her the wonders of photographic editing.

Finally, the inevitable shoe dropped: Jenny was doing homework at the kitchen table. I was cooking jambalaya from a cooking show recipe while watching a square faced Italian make family recipes on her cooking show. I had muted the commercial to tell Jenny about the time I tasted pistachio gelato for the first time when her mother appeared. She was white as a sheet and mumbled something incoherent before passing out. I checked her pulse. It was weak. We called 9-1-1.

Jenny began to cry as I followed the operator's directions. As soon as the EMTs arrived, they took her vitals and raced her to the hospital. We followed in my car while I followed the government protocol when trying to contact Duncan.

I couldn't reach Seymour or his wife at the farm. My parents met us at the hospital to take Jenny because I didn't know whom else that I could call. She tried to refuse leaving until she saw a man in a black suit and green tie with a woman in a navy power suit.

"That means Daddy can't come and they are going to be here with you," she whispered, eyes filled with tears. I hugged her so tightly that she could barely breathe.

"You can stay with me. My parents will stay with us," I offered.

"Okay," she cried. "Is my mom going to be okay?"

I looked over her head at my parents. They shrugged. My dad mouthed, "It's okay to tell her you don't know."

"I don't know, but we'll all find out together," she crawled into my lap like she was five instead of a preteen and lay her head under my chin.

The government duo introduced themselves as liaisons between Duncan and us. "You are new to the protocol, but we understand you have been briefed enough to know that the Professor is on a highly sensitive assignment, so you cannot contact him directly. We will ensure that he is contacted with all pertinent information."

Duncan explained later that they were also there for our safety. He never explained why a military intelligence lawyer would need protection for his family, but I guess a job title like that should explain enough. He also told me that they would have only interrupted his assignment if she had died and he needed to return for her funeral. Two government agents in a hospital did not exactly help the anxiety for a child or her temporary guardian. I was so grateful my parents lived in Brentwood.

The doctor later explained that Jenny's mother experienced something called "placental abruption." Her body went into distress due to that combined with preeclampsia. Unfortunately, the baby boy was stillborn at 29 weeks during the emergency C-section.

Other complications arose, and Jenny's mother almost didn't survive. While diagnoses and doctors swirled around us, all I focused on was the pale freckled face in my arms that I was supposed to anchor in reality amid this hospital storm.

Seymour and his wife showed up at the hospital. The government agents did not hurry to contact them to my knowledge or show up at their doorstep. Seymour and his wife tried to send me home with a promise to tend to Jenny. She clung to me without a word.

I glanced at my parents who noticed this response. Instead, I offered to take Jenny home with me. It was agreed. My parents started walking her to the exit while the government liaisons pulled me to the side away from the grandparents.

The female government agent said, "We have contacted the funeral home in case you can go ahead and begin making arrangements. We have in the paperwork that the in-laws are not to touch anything related to that."

My mouth opened and shut before managing to say, "Her little girl is ten feet away, and we don't even know for sure---"

The woman blushed immediately and touched her mouth, "No no no! I'm so sorry. I meant for the baby." I could feel the bile rising in my throat.

First Christopher and now this? "Oh. Oh dear," was all I could respond and grabbed her hand without thinking. I must have looked sick.

She squeezed my hand and placed her other on my shoulder like a coach in a pep talk, "I'm so sorry to spring that on you. You have been vetted and marked as trustworthy. At this point, I don't know if we can bring the Professor home because that's above my security level, but I do know that the mourning and grief in this are going to be important."

"I just buried my husband. I'm aware," I blurted, almost choking as tears sprang forth.

The woman's mouth dropped. For the first time I saw her humanity. Her lips went red while she paled. She looked at her partner, almost accusingly, "They didn't tell me that. I am so sorry for your loss, especially with all this."

I nodded as tears ran fresh down my face. "This summer."

Her poker face dropped and I could see the remorse streaked across her entire person. Rather than say anything else, this perfect stranger simply hugged me. I began crying, "Why the baby? The baby. Oh God the baby," and then almost in a sobbing prayer I repeated, "Not the mother too...Not the mother too..."

I have no concept of time of how long she held me. Seymour and his wife were nowhere to be seen. My parents were with Jenny at valet parking.

When I regained composure, she had mascara streaks down her face. We nodded and said nothing else. She returned to her post with her partner while I began wondering how to plan a funeral for an infant that wasn't even my own child.

Jenny's mother didn't stabilize for over a week, so we held a simple graveside service for the baby in a white casket covered in white and blue flowers. Once she was released from the hospital, I held her mother in my arms as she fell to the freshly sodded grave. I can't imagine the turmoil of basically passing out pregnant and awakening from the nightmare with no baby--inside or outside.

Duncan arrived two weeks after her discharge from the hospital. He was bleary-eyed with the news fresh after his debrief. I could hardly breathe in the guesthouse, nevertheless in their house upon his arrival. I quietly escaped back to New York for two weeks until Duncan had to leave again. He called me on his way to the airport.

"Is everything okay? Should I be flying to Bangkok in February?" I half-joked to him during the 3 AM wake up call.

Quite gravely he assured me that flights were fine to his knowledge. I sobered very quickly realizing that he might actually know that kind of thing. He asked if I could return to Nashville before my international appointments for February's fashion weeks.

I told him that I would, but cautiously I asked, "So, are your in-laws going to be there too? I will have to work from the house."

He said they would be there until I returned, but with Jenny in school, I'd simply be on call for his wife. We discussed some further details about the arrangements, and I realized that my role in their family had changed from renter to something more...valuable. When he clicked off the phone, I knew that there was potential for this to be our last conversation. Chilled, I threw myself into editing my latest project until the sun rose.

Duncan was gone much longer than planned. His wife curled up in bed around various bottles.

Daily, my job became running the house and trying to get her out of the bed. Seymour and his wife put everything at their farm in the hands of their "house manager " and planted themselves in a spare bedroom in the main house.

Feeling released of responsibility with them around for February, I cycled guilt-free back and forth to New York, Bangkok, Paris, and Nashville. I brought Jenny souvenirs, food, and stories. My flights and work out-of-town continued past February fashion weeks. Suddenly it was spring and Duncan had still not returned from his unknown location...

    Three lightning bugs blinked and winked. Jenny and I chased them with Mason jars and laughter. My cats stared motionless at us from the window. Their eyes blinked and winked chartreuse like the lightning bugs. I had forgotten my camera in the studio in the guesthouse. I itched to capture her laugh, those baby girl cheeks, and those freckles...

    In that moment, my heart stopped aching. I didn't miss Christopher. My job didn't matter. The Franklin estate had officially gone off the market due to lack of sales and the housing market crash. My suitcase remained empty instead of packed. All I had was an infinite amount of time with a twelve year old that wanted to catch lightning bugs and asked if I would join her.

    We chased them and tripped over our feet. We laughed as she collided into me during an epic dive. She caught it! We stayed piled in our collision heap and watched the bug blink and flutter in the jar. The yard seemed to fill with lightning bugs to match the stars beginning to poke through the sky.

    She let the bug go. We watched it join the summer dance as she shifted to the ground beside me. We were covered in grass stains and dirt. She dropped the jar beside her as we lay side by side, staring at the sky. I held my Mason jar on my chest. A lightning bug landed on it! I gasped and pointed. She gasped and clapped her hands on her mouth to suppress a giggle. I tried not to laugh at her laughing. Finally, we burst. The bug shot away; it seemed startled in a jagged flight-pattern away from us. I moved the jar to the ground beside me as we both rolled facing each other and giggling.

"You should have seen your face!"
"You kept making me laugh!"
"We lost the bugs!"
"You're a mess!"
"No you're a mess!"

She pushed my shoulder. I fell onto my back dramatically before cutting my face back at her with a serious expression. She laughed and snuggled next to me. She grabbed my hand in the way that only little children do.

I thought I'd finally found a home.
I thought...
I thought that...
Maybe, I was home...

A voice from the main house yelled. It sounded like Seymour, but it was difficult to tell. Jenny sighed, "But!" The voice's response cut toward us, but we were caught in our lightning bug jars and the summer haze. I squeezed her hand.

We sat up with leaves and grass in our hair. "She's coming!" I yelled for her. She smiled. I dusted her off while she dusted me off. Her overalls were getting too short, and the pigtails fell lopsided. She giggled. I helped her remove the hair bands. All at once she hugged me. I almost didn't hug her back because I was so surprised.

"Thank you for today," came her muffled voice.

I patted her head and hugged her. "No little one, thank you," I managed to say. She pulled away and grinned to reveal a mouth full of white little teeth.

The voice from the back porch called again. We both yelled. She started running to the back of the house, but I called her name and was running toward her with the Mason jars. She yanked her hair in a ponytail while turning around to meet me. I handed her the jars, and she made a silly face at forgetting them. At a slower pace, she hugged the jars and jogged toward the house.

I stood on the back lawn and watched her. When she entered the lower back door, she paused and waved a jar at me. I waved back at her. Above her on the back porch, a solitary lump of shadow separated into two people. The light on the house eaves shined behind the figures, which kept their individual features masked.

Seymour's shape was the only masculine figure in our consistent world. I could easily pinpoint which one was most likely him. He raised a hand at me. Maybe he thought I was waving to him? I waved and walked to the guesthouse, chilled despite the summer heat.

I entered my house--the guesthouse--and attempted to not trip over the cats. They had tired of eyeballing the lightning bugs. Hunger seemed much more imperative. I hurried to the kitchen to fix their dinner before they decided I might be appetizing. Once they happily ate their perfectly plated canned meals, I was free to find myself dinner.

I rifled through take-out and delivery menus and found myself wishing for 24-hour barbecue delivery. In the middle of the stack was an invitation to the Gala. I had completely forgotten about it, and it was the next day. I groaned out loud to the cats, "Why EVEN go?"

The cats didn't bother looking at me. At least I had a dress no one in Nashville had seen.

Bummed I ordered pizza and curled up with my laptop and my favorite date: work. If I could create something beautiful, maybe my insides would stop hurting for a few minutes...at least...that's what I told myself.

I worked on a project until I fell asleep on my laptop. I received a call from one of my assistant photographers in Manhattan. He was panicked because pink slips had officially gone through some of the departments. Sobered, I calmed him down and promised to be in the city by Monday instead of conference calling for staff meeting.

"They can't do a web magazine without great photography, right?" he pleaded.

"That's true, but who knows what that means for our jobs," I replied softly.

He sobered and asked if I could be his reference. I assured him I would work on a reference letter to have in his hand when I walked in the office Monday. He then gasped, "Really? You...you would do that?"

Gently I said, "Corbin, you know my story of coming into this business. It was completely grace and favor. What kept me employed is that I work harder than anyone else. You have the talent and the work ethic. Trust me. It would be my delight to refer you to anyone for any job."

"Wow," he whispered. "You've never said anything like that before now."

"What? That I got into the business on grace and favor?" I chuckled.

"No," he swallowed. "That I have talent."

I started to drop the phone with my jaw. Had I become like my mentor--so hardened and fanatical that my assistants didn't realize they had talent until I called them to take a picture like he had me do of Nicole in my Mona Lisa smile?

"I'm not saying that you aren't kind, but you've never said I have talent. That--that means a lot. With everything happening, I've started to wonder…"

"Pink slips and people losing everything do make you start to rethink things. It's normal. You have talent and work ethic. Otherwise, I wouldn't have kept you at the magazine this long."

He laughed and said only one name, "I forgot about Katelyn."

The laughter set us both free for a moment to reminisce about the absolute worst temp ever assigned to us. She couldn't make coffee. She had terrible number issues. She had no concept of lighting or photography terms. She broke the copier and misfiled EVERYTHING, but she could rock a mini skirt, red lipstick, and blonde hair no matter the year or season. She lasted approximately two working days.

When she was giggling with the male models about how oiled their skin was, I lost it. "Since you can't do the job assigned to you, get out of here this instant!" I raged very quietly, barely above a whisper, in her ear before pointing to the door.

I meant out of the studio. She never returned to the building. She's on some MTV reality show now so no hard feelings, I'm sure. (Providentially, she met the producer in the elevator as she left).

When I got off the phone, I began writing a list of everyone who worked in my department. Next to each name, I wrote the connections I could call to ask in some favors to see about getting them interviews in the city. The end was rapidly approaching, and I wasn't even thinking about where I would go to for my next job post.

My phone buzzed with a calendar reminder for the Frist Gala and my hair appointment. Someone had paid attention when I agreed to this silent auction and benefit. Rather than cancel the appointment, I hurried to the salon and soaked my thoughts in shampoo, Argon oil, and beauty shop gossip. I had never been to this salon before, so it was fun to hear them discussing the latest fashion. Out of nowhere, I found myself talking about fashion week in Bangkok.

"Girl, what were you doin' in Bangkok?" she asked. The salon was empty because it was a rainy, dreary day, so most clients had canceled. Two of the other hairdressers sat in chairs on either side of me to join our chat.

I laughed. I really wasn't in New York. "I'm a photographer."

They all had experience doing hair for high fashion catwalks and hair shows. I had made my appointment as "Annice MacKensie," so when I grabbed my laptop and said, "I'm Annice Wall," they all three got eyes as round as dinner platters.

I began to pull up *Best Dressed*'s website, but one of the girls had raced to her station and back with a magazine filled with marked pages. She had a two page spread open as she raced to me. "This is you!"

I laughed. The photograph was of Nicole who I had used during my infamous "Mona Lisa" wedding shoot. This editorial was actually from a more recent session in Italy.

"Yes, I took that photograph," I smiled and pointed to my name in white against the navy along the edge of the page.

Rather than be bombarded with questions about the models, these girls wanted to know how hair and makeup worked at the shoots. For a moment, I grew lost in the delight of the magic of fashion. We continued to talk through an unscheduled manicure-pedicure, and then they even did my make up. Fortunately, I had my dress in the car, so my new salon "besties" grabbed it for me so that I could change and not be late to downtown for the gala. The dress didn't have a label, so when I whispered the designer, I thought they were going to pass out all over each other. He only designs for six foot and taller skinny models, but for me, he custom-designed a plum, floor length gown.

Babs, my hairdresser, said softly when I entered the salon from the bathroom in my dress, "And this lady, girls, is Manhattan meets Nashville in the flesh."

I blushed and hugged my new friends before racing through the drizzle to meet destiny. At the time, I had no idea that destiny was an introverted restaurateur with puppy bright eyes and a horrible ability to maintain conversation.

I had forgotten to order a car and driver, so I pulled up to the valet for the gala in my red and white '66 Chevy C10. The truck was the only splurge I made after Christopher's death. I knew some guys in town that restored antique cars. I saw the truck in someone's yard near Five Points in East Nashville. It was white and blue and rust. The engine wouldn't even turn over, but I was in love.

I called up Charlie, remembering him from Christopher's funeral. "I don't care the price. Let's have fun with this. I just bought a '66 Chevy C10 that doesn't run and may be rusted through," is all I said before he guffawed in my ear. "Honey, paint me a picture and we'll create something beautiful in the middle of your grief mess."

He was the only person willing to call out straight to me what I was doing, but a widower himself, he understood.

The valet whistled as he opened my door, "Ma'am, this ain't the kinda car I expected, but she sure does rumble! Was she in the family?"

I smiled proudly and looked at his nametag, "Scotty, I adopted this old truck into the family with some help from Charlie at Classic Trucks 'n' Stuff."

Scotty grinned, "I thought I recognized this old lady. Charlie's my uncle."

Of course he is, I smiled and shook my head.

Another gentleman hurried to my side with an umbrella as Scotty handed me a valet ticket.

"You may want to save your hair with this," he said as he held the black umbrella over us.

"Oh well thanks. Hi. I'm Anni. Who are you?" I tucked my clutch under my arm and extended my hand toward him while looking for a nametag. I thought he was a valet.

He blushed. "Peter."

We shook hands while striding to the doors. I could barely keep up with him in my heels, so I couldn't even get a question out for conversation without sounding like a winded seal. He grabbed the door for me as he shut the umbrella with one hand. I stepped into the lobby where I saw Alice, the museum director, engaging and directing each guest toward the fullness of the Gala. She saw me enter and waved me over to meet the elderly couple caught in her welcoming web. I smiled and held a finger up because I was going to thank my umbrella escort, yet when I turned to find him, Peter had disappeared in his black and grey pinstriped suit and burgundy bow tie.

Miffed, I smoothed my dress while continuing to look around for the suddenly disappeared escort before engaging Alice in the networking drudgery I had anticipated as the latest large donor to an amazing museum.

"Dr. and Mrs. Campbell, it's my pleasure to introduce to you Mrs. Annice Mackensie," Alice flashed brilliantly white teeth that disguised the ridiculous amount of coffee I had seen her consume in prior weeks.

"It's a pleasure," we chorused while shaking hands and then laughed.

While chuckling herself, Alice said, "I wanted to make certain to introduce you all because Dr. Campbell is now a retired neurosurgeon and he assists his wife in her bridal and formalwear boutique. The shop has been a mainstay in Nashville for years and they were delighted to hear from Wendell that you are assisting in creating a high fashion photography show with some of your contacts in New York."

"Oh Wendell is too kind," I could feel my face flushing. "I have a few friends that have wanted to collaborate for a show, so they have agreed to open it in New York and do it here as well. We are also hoping to showcase the work in LA and Chicago. Wendell is going to co-curate in every city. It's much more a launch for his career than mine. I'm simply a photographer."

Dr. Campbell patted my arm like an old grandfather and winked, "I'm told you aren't simply a photographer."

Mrs. Campbell grinned, grabbed my arm, and began guiding me into the party. "Yes Mrs. Anni, I knew your mother-in-law, God rest her soul, so I am quite familiar that you are actually the Mrs. Annie Wall."

The look of surprise was unmistakable. They both laughed like conspiring school children on the playground. They swept me into the middle of the gala and silent auction where I was introduced (and in some cases reintroduced) to Nashville's elite.

Basically, I was dragged through the silent auction and passed from arm to arm of ladies who were "simply devastated by Christopher and his mother's passing so close together." I even had to go through "the loveliness" and "beautiful tribute" that they called the funerals. I suddenly wanted to drink whiskey. I don't drink. We had only made it through the beginning of cocktail hour.

I slipped over to the bar for a coke only to see that one of the evening's signature drinks related to the "Mackensie collection." Dear Lord, what on earth had I gotten myself into this time? Seriously? I remember praying while still ordering a Coke without ice.

"Not a drinker?" came a familiar voice.

"I sip wine in Europe because it's custom, but no. I really like water," I said looked up and up at the very strong man to my left. His suit was custom tailored to hang properly from his broad shoulders. "Well hello Umbrella Man."

He smiled through what looked like two days of stubble. "Hello Anni. Nice to see you again."

"I agree," I smiled.

He didn't order anything from the bartender and seemed to watch the room like a bouncer or security detail. Then he began dialing on his phone.

"Military?" I offered.

"What?" he looked stunned that I was still standing next to him. People were beginning to be ushered into the dinner.

"I asked--"

"No not military. Just a second," he put the phone to his ear. "Yeah. We're going to need three more meals. Make sure they are steak because it looks like a majority of men, but prepare one extra chicken just in case."

Great. The one person I'm comfortable with is working the party, I thought glumly.

I decided that meant I was most likely going to be trapped at dinner with more people that knew my in-laws and would want to talk about funerals.

"Sorry about that," he smiled awkwardly and began fidgeted with his collar and sleeve cuffs. "It's a big launch for us to cater this caliber of meal in Nashville. My restaurant in Atlanta has done a few big events, but this is my new Nashville chef's debut here. She's a nervous wreck."

I must have made a face when he said 'she' because he immediately began backtracking, "We aren't married or anything. I hired her because I own the restaurant. Wow that sounds pompous."

We froze and awkwardly looked at the bar as if wine or a nonalcoholic signature beverage might save us. I liked that he had no clue who I was, so I figured that I could give it another go.

"Usually when women get nervous they need something to hold onto as a pivot point to anchor the moment. Sometimes that's a hug or a pep talk or a cup of tea. It helps bring reality from a whirlwind to a steady pace," I offered. "She might need a pep talk."

He nodded for a moment. "I can do that."

I smiled hopefully, "Sure. You own two restaurants and a catering business. Sure you can."

"Three restaurants. I'm opening a barbecue joint next week to make four."

"Wow. Four is impressive and you're so young."

He shrugged. "I have an excellent team of investors and staff. We do amazing work together." I took a sip of my coke.

Before either of us could make another comment, he simply walked toward what I could only imagine was the prepping area for the food. The bartender laughed, "I guess he was finished with that conversation."

I looked at the bartender and shrugged, miffed again, "I guess so."

The museum Gala was everything I expected it to be since I wasn't behind a camera. I sat awkwardly making conversation with a surgeon and his wife to my left and a widower with his much younger new wife to my right. We were all new donors as well as newly relocated to Nashville.

I had to make a small speech about the Mackensie collection. Alice mentioned Christopher's death, so I was the tearful widow talking about art and feeling like a royal ninny (as my grandmother would have said).

I ended up one of the last to leave because everyone wanted to talk to me. The collection was opening for exhibit the next day, so everyone at the gala had a preview that evening. Thus, almost every person wanted to speak with me about the "generous collection" I had added to Nashville's growing artistic center. Even Peter the restaurateur spoke to me as I was walking to the valet.

"We meet again," I smiled.

"That speech about your husband and the art was lovely," he blurted.

I could see instantly his grimace and I laughed, "Thanks. Art and death kind of go hand-in-hand."

He rubbed his face as if attempting to erase his embarrassment. "I guess sometimes. Well, nice to meet you," he held out his hand.

"You too Peter," I shook his hand and we both looked down and laughed. We were attempting to hand one another our business cards in the handshake.

"I guess we can't both be subtle," he laughed.

"I guess not," I laughed too. "Thanks for this. I'm excited to try your barbecue after tonight's amazing meal."

He blinked. "Great."

I held up his card, "At your new barbeque restaurant?"

He chuckled and turned red. "Right. I hope to see you there soon."

"I do too," I shocked myself in replying while handing the valet my ticket.

T he valet gleefully skipped to retrieve my truck. I could hear the engine roar before he even pulled to the curb. I must have had the most fun car to drive for the valets all night. I turned to ask when the restaurant was open and if they delivered, but again, Peter disappeared.

I chuckled to myself and thought, *He's going to be an interesting friend.*

I climbed into the cab of the pick-up, but I found myself glancing back at the sidewalk in hopes of a final glance of Peter's broad form. He was gone, but I surprised myself by being disappointed. I shook off the emotion and focused on the drive to the guesthouse and plans for my trip back up to New York.

When I walked into the *Best Dressed* offices, employees scattered into twos and threes to discuss my arrival. Everyone knew that I was telecommuting and had a made a big push to save money by having more employees telecommute even a few days a week as well as push for more digital communication rather than paper. Since my proposal, we had higher productivity in four months than we had ever experienced and saved thousands of dollars in our electrical and supply budgets. This also meant that if I had an unscheduled arrival for a normal staff meeting, something was about to happen.

As senior photography editor, I was actually the youngest and most inexperienced editor on staff. *Best Dressed* was a pet project by one of my mentor's friends, so when he heard about it, he threw my name in the hat rather than his own.

"I'm getting too old and I like picking and choosing my own projects," he had told me when I was tapped for the job. Wisely, he understood that I needed structure to be groomed into navigating high fashion politics while he could be a temperamental artist and drive editors nuts all over the world.

We both figured it would be a short-term gig because high fashion was not sought by the Internet social demographic, but *BD* proved that great writing and photography could change the World Wide Web and the accessibility of high fashion to the masses.

When the economy crashed, our site actually jumped in numbers because we were completely paperless. A small membership fee provided access to a majority of our material, but with the advertising, even our free component jumped in revenue.

I was rather proud of our magazine and accepted nothing less than excellence. I became known as the "how can we do this better" editor, which caused headaches and last minute scrambles for deadlines but (in the end) some really fantastic work.

As I headed to the photography studio, I bumped into a very tall thin man clutching his laptop and a fistful of manila folders.

"Oh hello Anni," he patted me on the back as if our bump was actually an awkward hug.

I looked up at him, "Oh hello Trey."

He started to continue walking, but I stopped him. "Trey, walk with me to the studio."

He swallowed. Trey was from accounting. He was the last person left by our parent magazine in our accounting office, and he looked pale. We chatted in hushed tones to the studio where I typically set up office now that I was telecommuting.

"Trey, I had on of my assistants call me at home. That's why I'm here. There's no pink slips being issued or terrifying hammers being thrown. My team is freaked out, so I want to know from the numbers guy what the numbers are saying," I said while shutting the door.

My heels clicked and echoed across the cement studio floor. I sat in my favorite ergonomic desk chair and grabbed my mug of tea. Corbin must have made it because he was the only one who knew to anticipate my arrival after our phone call, but I hadn't seen him in my walk down the halls.

It dawned on me that Clara, my administrative assistant, hadn't appeared either. I looked at my desk again and saw the letter of resignation sitting there with fresh ink.

Trey swallowed, squeaked trying to respond, and then swallowed again. I smiled and gestured to the folding chair next to my wooden barn table that I used as a desk. He adjusted his tie and smoothly his sports coat.

"This magazine was a pet-project. We lasted longer than anyone expected. With the economy crashing, people are pulling their advertising from everywhere. You've seen how other magazines are getting cut and absorbed by the parent company," he paused and looked at his left hand.

I grabbed a bottle of water from the bucket under my desk and handed it to him. "Trey, if you are looking at your wedding band, this tells me two things."

I looked up at me startled. "I am."

I smiled, but sadly. "This tells me that you are-- one--worried, and two, you are worried because your wife is pregnant again."

He gulped. "How did you--?"

I flashed back for a second to my unexpected pregnancy early in my and Christopher's marriage. We didn't even know I could get pregnant. It looked like an act of God, and I remember Christopher making that same face when we went to an obstetrician appointment and the heartbeat was concerning. We lost the baby three days later. I never told anyone, but I'll never forget that face.

"You aren't going to lose everything. I promise. You are a CPA. We've been here from the beginning--the youngest idiots to take a chance on a six month promise that turned into longer," I said, and we smiled sadly at one another. "We were first hires which is why we will probably be last fired, but Trey, you have enough experience to get a great job out of this industry. Your family will be fine."

He swallowed. "I needed that. I just really like this job. Who else has to figure out how to explain 500 plastic frogs on a tax form? It was always interesting," he stopped. We both realized he said 'was.'

"So, you have another job lined up then?"

"The parent company actually wants to move me into their department, but my wife wants to leave the city, so I accepted a job in Portland. It's not as glamorous, but we will be near family," his eyes smiled with hope.

"That will be great."

He showed me pictures of the ultrasound and his other two girls. I found myself sharing with him how I couldn't sell the Franklin estate, so I was trying to figure out what to do. I was considering buying out the farm next to ours because they were in major financial hardship. I could literally rescue them if I bought the house and property before they had to foreclose.

"Their house is seriously the perfect wedding spot. They have had a few people do wedding shoots there too," I laughed while explaining how the Sizemores loved lavish parties. (Their Versailles-inspired Halloween party still gets mentioned at the high-end charity benefits in town. Everyone rented costumes, and a few showed up in Louis XVI stylized chariots with horses. The party hosted 324 people over three days)!

I could see the numbers clicking in Trey's head as shared their difficulty in being able to maintain the grounds or high end parties in their retirement. "If you turned it into an event hub, you would make back your investment within two years. You're known for the wedding dress Mona Lisa. People will flock to you."

"Really? I—"

Corbin, my main assistant photographer, opened the studio door. "The meeting will begin in five minutes."

Trey and I looked at each other and nodded. As we stood and walked to the staff meeting, we both knew what we had to do. I saw Clara carrying two empty boxes toward me, which was the direction of her desk. I nodded solemnly and grabbed her elbow. "I saw your letter. Please don't leave before I can take you to lunch," I whispered. She blinked, shrugged her shoulders to her ears, and looked at me almost from a puppy-like 45-degree angle. "Of--of course."

All the editorial staff sat at the conference table--literally all of us. Three-fourths of us had chosen to telecommute a majority of our time, so conference call staff meetings had become the normal protocol. As I looked around at each face, I could almost see the names of who called each one of us floating above our heads. My heart was warmed by this realization.

In this economic crisis that scrolled in our news reports at alarming rates, the realization that people were at stake had come to the forefront for so many of us in management. While CEOs and Presidents of companies were being lambasted for firing hundreds and thousands of employees, many high and low on the totem poles were quietly trying to figure out how to keep employees while cutting costs in an effort to save families, marriages, jobs, and children's futures.
Kevin, our Editor-in-Chief, sipped his green tea as he eyed each of us before checking his watch. Precisely on the hour, Kevin's assistant Jan cued the projector and the presentation.

"What a pleasant surprise that we are all here and not needing to do one of those annoying conference calls," he looked pointedly at me.

"Annoying but they work," I shot back without thinking.

No one made a sound.

Kevin cleared his throat. "Anyway, I've been speaking with Portia and Sydney…"

The temperature in the room disappeared. He turned his back to us, and we all looked at each other. Portia and Sydney ran the empire. We knew that. They literally held the keys to every job in the corporate tree from our parent company to the other sister and brother magazines we shared virtual shelves with in the marketplace.

"…so they want to hear your ideas on what we can do that's edgy. I know Anni has suggested we move into posting more videos and incorporating a behind the scenes, what are they called, Anni?"

"A blog, Kevin?" I arched my eyebrows. These were ideas I had pitched before Christopher had died.

"Yeah, so what are other things we can do?"

Trey piped up. "And it has to be on a shoestring budget. They aren't giving us any additional resources to boost these things. We are almost halfway through the fiscal year for our magazine so we are stuck with literally all that's left, and we just had a major advertiser pull their ad this morning from our circulation to cut their budget."

Questions started shooting out of everyone's mouths:

"Is our brand strong enough without advertising?"

"Can we push a grassroots movement again to recharge our brand?"

"What if we made sure things didn't look perfect? It would be edgy and different. Movies are already playing with those effects."

"Can we survive without additional funds from the parents?"

"Why are they pulling funds from us? We fund revenue for them!"

"Hush."

At first they didn't hear me, so I repeated myself as though I was talking to Jenny while her mother was in the hospital and she cried on the sofa at a grocery store commercial about family.

"Hush."

Everyone looked at me. I remember I was wearing the most perfect silk dress and my favorite heels. I never wore heels or a dress to work, especially in the studio. It was easier to take photographs in pants so that I could move modestly, especially if I needed to get on the floor or a ladder for the perfect angle. It dawned on me that must be part of why people whispered.

I crossed my arms and looked straight at Kevin. "Are we really going to jump at this charade, Kevin?"

He started to speak but I waved my finger at him like a Southern grandmother and clucked, "Tsk tsk tsk. Now sit."

He flushed red and started to point to send me out of the office. I didn't move. Trey looked right at him, "You know she is right."

Humbled, Kevin sat.

"It has been a pleasure to work and learn from each of you, and I can tell you that we all know when someone is blowing smoke. Sometimes we laugh it off and ignore it. Other times we call it out. Today is a day to be real. They are pulling the budget because they want their own job security. We are all here because I bet everyone of you had someone call you this weekend asking you what to do," I paused.

Everyone nodded, including Kevin and Jan. I continued while unfolding a piece of paper from a yellow legal pad. I had folded, unfolded, written, and refolded that sheet of paper countless times since my phone call with Corbin.

I showed them the list of names on the sheet of paper while I said: "This is every person still currently in my department including Linda who cleans the studio. You know she's the only person I trust in that space. Beside each name is what they do, how long they have worked for me down to the number of days, and what they are capable of doing. The remnant I am left with is a stellar cast, but people, they are going to absorb us because we have done a BRILLIANT job of proving that high fashion has a place on the internet. They just want this pie for themselves. Now, you can help your people assimilate into the absorption or help them find jobs, but the honest truth is that we aren't going to have jobs by the time these ideas come to fruition because Portia and Sydney and Kevin are going to use them to re-launch the parent brand."

Everyone grew quiet. Sue piped up, "You really know the days?"

"I write everyone's start date in my planner so that if they make it a year I can celebrate them. It doesn't take much math to figure out the days," I shrugged.

She shook her head.

"Trey, seriously, tell us how long we probably have even if we did the boost ideas ourselves?" Alex asked quietly.

"Three or four months," Trey replied so softly we almost couldn't hear him.

Kevin chortled on his tea. "Are you joking?"

Trey shook his head and held up one of his manila folders. "I've accepted an offer in Portland, Oregon. I have my letter of resignation here. The numbers can't be crunched any further if they keep taking our budget and our people."

The color drained from Kevin's face.

"So let's call this what this is. It was a slow-burn take-over, but we were a success all the way to the end. If you want to stay and fight to prove me wrong, so be it, but I will also give you, Kevin, my letter of resignation by the end of the week."

I pushed in my chair and began to leave the meeting. In silence, we one-by-one stood and left Kevin and Jan alone in the conference room. I grabbed every photography department employee I could see and told them to meet me in the studio.

"Who wants to blow off for lunch?" I asked once they were all assembled.

Corbin asked softly, "This isn't a 'here's lunch but you are all fired' invitation is it?"

I laughed. "Nope. I announced my resignation today and want to celebrate. Clara has also found a fantastic opportunity in Paris, so we need to celebrate her too. I'm buying so let's be ridiculous."

They all cheered. Clara excitedly phoned in a favor to my favorite chef who had a table waiting for us. I had him make a special box that I could bring to Linda our cleaning lady. I spoke to each of them privately and handed them letters. I spent most of my Sunday afternoon bothering contacts' weekend plans to secure interviews and/or jobs for all my employees at the magazine. I told each one what I had done and handed each my reference letter for them. Since Clara already had a job, I handed her a reference letter and said, "In case you need it in the future." Tears sprang to her eyes.

When I left the city at the end of that week, I took the last of my belongings back with me to Tennessee. All my friends took me out almost every night to celebrate my new chapter, and that's when I pitched to Jack the idea of becoming my event coordinator if things worked out with purchasing the neighboring property. His wife said yes for him, "Hire us both. Relocating would be amazing. It's a dream opportunity for both of us."

(After the property purchase from the Sizemores went through, I sent Trey what I called a 'finder's fee.' He called choked up and said, "Just don't forget you and Christopher's dream to take care of street kids. I know it fell apart since he died and you left Manhattan and the church there, but something can happen later. God doesn't plant a seed He won't grow." As he did in Manhattan, Trey always knew exactly how to speak truth in the best possible way).

As I unpacked my belongings from my final trip related to *BD,* I found myself lingering over the things I held as essentials there. Borrowing my mentor's flat for all those months when I stayed in NY, I felt my existence as a nomad while traveling from job to job with landing places in Nashville and NY. This trip sealed the end of a chapter in my career in a way I hadn't expected, but it also pointed me to a new home. Yet, there I sat in a guesthouse, which was quite pointedly not truly my home, while I owned a property fully in my name that I couldn't bear to live in alone.

The essentials of a traveler are few and far between because travelers learn what to anticipate bringing is not as obvious. Toiletries are often provided or easily purchased in destinations. Really, you can travel with 1-2 sets of clothes and purchase while you are traveling. No, the essentials are personal items like certain cameras, books, cords, and that perfect pair of sunglasses. A traveler's essentials bring home with the person.

I sat on the bed with a shoebox of letters, unframed photographs, postcards, and small journals. My hands shook. Rather than open the box, I bent over and slid it under the bed. Taking a deep breath, I went to the kitchen to ignore a fresh wave of grief over the life and career I walked away from over the course of a week. I opened the fridge. It was empty except for a single bottle of barbecue sauce with a note. My hands shook as I picked them up. They had arrived the day I returned from my trip to New York a few days prior. The messenger was a very sweet man with the most hopeful eyes I had ever seen. I took a deep breath and opened the note again:

Dear Anni-

This is a token of my appreciation for being so kind to me at the Frist Gala. I apologize for my foot-in-the-mouth comment, but you were beautiful. It trips a man up when he is captivated. It's a chemical thing; I promise. If you choose, enjoy this with a piece of chicken and your cats, or, if you are willing, share it with someone. Preferably me.

Thank you again,
Peter

I smiled, left the note on the counter to stare at for another few days, and called for take-out. I placed it back in the fridge with a door full of assorted juices and water bottles. It looked lonely there, much like he had looked at the gala.

Later that night, when I crawled into bed, I realized it had been hours since I thought of Christopher. I pulled our wedding picture from beneath his pillow and began to cry. Maybe it was guilt for beginning to move on from him? Maybe it was relief? Maybe both?

I awoke the next morning to a phone call from Seymour asking if I could run some errands and take Jenny with me. It was a Monday and school holiday. I remember being surprised Jenny hadn't been at my door all weekend since I was back in town until that phone call. When the grandparents were around, Jenny seemed to disappear into the house or was out with Seymour. He explained that he and his wife needed to leave the city for a few days. That meant I was back on duty, but I found myself delighted for a change of pace from wallowing in memories and brainstorm lists for project ideas to maintain my career. Jenny practically skipped with me as we went through the grocery store.

"Who took that picture?"
"Ellen von Unwerth."
"Okay, what about that one?"
"Afanador."
"That wasn't English."
"That's his last name."
"Okay, what's his first name."
"Ruvin."
"You made that up!"

"I did not."
"Okay, what about this one?"
"Me."
"What!"

She snatched the magazine off the shelf and held it practically under her nose. "You took this, like for real?"

"Yes," I laughed. "They're *Best Dressed*'s parent-magazine actually. I've been senior photographer for BD for a while, but I still do my own projects because it's an online magazine. This cover was one of my other projects."

"We're buying it," she tossed the magazine in the grocery cart as though she was footing the bill.

I pulled it out, "Jen, it's not on the list--"

She started running in place with her hands folded like she was praying or pleaded. She hurried to me with the saddest frown and biggest eyes she could muster. "Please please please please please please please please please please...."

"Look," I stopped the cart. She stretched her frown into a half-grin. "If you have the money to buy it yourself, you can." She collapsed into a genuine frown. "Or you can see the reject shots I still have back at the house?"

"The house!" she declared and hugged me. "Can there be ice cream?"

I laughed, "At my house, there is always ice cream."

She clapped gleefully and pranced down the aisle. I kept the magazine in the cart, but I slid it under the frozen pizzas I was going to purchase. When I pulled the magazine out of the bags at the guesthouse later, she screamed and danced around the kitchen with it clutched to her chest. I popped two of the pizzas in the oven and laughed at her. She fell asleep on my couch looking at photo shoots I had edited and projects that would be coming out in the next year. She asked question after question, soaking up all the details of how the fashion world operated.

That Monday lingered as one of those golden moments, which began more and more time together in both the main and guesthouses. I would move laundry while she did homework and her mother would disappear for seemingly days at a time. My presence scooted Seymour and his wife to their own home.

The event facility project brought Jenny's mother out of her room. In an effort to get her some sunshine, I would spread out all my design samples on the back porch picnic table in the morning. The summer heat wasn't quite unbearable at that hour, so we'd drink coffee and brainstorm together.

Jenny would join us with her homemade strawberry orange juice. Color actually began to return to both of them for the first time in months.

Peter would often call and show up with barbecue for lunch while I consulted with my contractor and interior designer. Peter would have Jenny laughing about stories from his restaurant kitchens and always end it with, "And that's why you aren't allowed to work in food service." This was typically because he would realize he shared something inappropriate or offensive, but her laugh cackled which made her eyes sparkle and cheeks turn pink.

FOUND

If my life was a movie, this is where the story would end. We all worked through our grief and eventually found our happily ever after because our hope floated or some nonsense.

Real life doesn't work that way. Real life is carrying an armload of laundry and finding Jenny's mother standing next to a filled bathtub with an open pill bottle in one hand and empty glass of Jack in the other. Real life is praying out loud in words you don't even know as you run to her, throwing the laundry into a slow motion rain of color, and praying, maybe even in English, that she hadn't taken the pills. Real life is becoming a temporary guardian every time Jenny's dad had to leave on assignment because her mother was checked into a private hospital to properly deal with her grief and depression. Real life is realizing the glorious summer was about to end with school restarting and Jenny had barely left her house to be with friends unless she knew her "beloved grandparents" were going to be back in the main house. Real life is filled with moments you stuff down in the steam trunk of your memory baggage because you can't bare to face the truth you cannot change. Some truths you cannot change are the truths you bury deep in your heart and pray that they change you. They are the words of life that explode breath and blood and electricity throughout your entire being. Those words are not the kind you bury in a steam trunk. The truths you bury in a steam trunk are the truths you don't have the capacity to deal with properly...

For months that turned into years, I would pull out those truths and memories and moments. Sometimes they would smack me in the face without warning, taking my breath away from me, but mostly in the middle of the night, I would dream of the situations I had no authority to change.

Of all the moments and the hindsight debates of what I should have seen, what stands out is the moment I did see. It is a moment that was never clouded by other memories because it is the time when everything as I knew it changed.

Prior to that moment, the pizza and movie sleepovers on nights she "should have been" with her grandparents felt like rewards for driving to school, pressing her uniform, and making rue for (her favorite) jambalaya. At the time, I couldn't see how those moments were different than an invite to hear her read the poems she entered into a poetry contest or request to teach her friends how to make pasta and baklava in the main house when they had a fall break sleepover extravaganza. Those memories are simply sentences and chapters in the lost story buried in my memory baggage of a time when all the pieces of my person were strewn about multiple houses and apartments in multiple states. Yet, those ordinary moments...that doing life together...with all her hugs and giggles and lightning bugs...those were the balm to the gaping wound that was my heart and the stitches that sewed back together my scattered person.

Her quickly growing girl to woman form reminded me that life changed, seasons changed, and there were people who needed me to be a champion, not a wailing widow. Because of her, I said "yes" to dates with Peter and tentatively dreamed of a life with someone other than Christopher and my cats. Each "yes" turned into "yes" in other areas of my life so that gradually even the nightmares of Christopher's car twisted beneath an 18-wheeler began to lessen and lessen. My time in the guesthouse had extended far beyond the original 6 months, but by the time my eyes were opened, I didn't realize that my time there was about to abruptly end.

What preceded the moment was a walk into the main house with soup and an idea. Jenny's mom arrived home a couple weeks prior. Her skin was lightly browned and her cheeks carried some pink with new freckles. Her eyes were still dulled gray-green, but she smiled. Jenny raced into the kitchen when she smelled the soup and immediately began diving into the pot with a bowl and ladle. I turned to her mother and said, "So I've been trying to decide what to do next career wise. The event facility is running well, but my heart is still photography. I've shot quite a few freelance things and I've taken some writing jobs here and there. The show I did with Wendell was a huge success, and I've had some friends that are gallery owners begging me to open my own show, so here's the pitch: Would you be one of my models?"

Stunned, Jenny's mother open and shut her mouth. Jenny answered for her, "Yes of course she would! That's awesome!"

We all laughed and ate soup while brainstorming how to do it. I decided I wanted to use their spare bedroom that would have been the baby's room. It had become a hodge-podge for storage, so it could easily be turned into whatever type of space I wanted. We cleared out the room to create a blank slate for set up, but the lighting was absolutely terrible. While in New York, I had relied heavily on the magazine for resources, but I still had enough of my own lights, modifiers, and equipment to set up a proper shoot. Jenny stood in as my assistant while I shot pictures of her mother for the better part of an afternoon.

By the end of the shoot, Jenny's mother was laughing. Her eyes brightened to a crystal green. Her throat was pink, and her hands moved effortless as we spoke, positioned, repositioned, and clicked away the day. The portrait I actually used was of her looking away from the camera, eyelids closed, and she was holding a handkerchief to her mouth. I managed to capture a single tear on her cheek. The handkerchief was monogrammed with the initials of the son who died. I titled it "After grief is a lie." Neither Jenny nor her mother realized I was still shooting. I heard Jenny say, "Mom, you are so beautiful," as her mother said, "It's still so hard." I stopped the shoot. We embraced in silence. Her mother slipped to her room for some time alone while Jenny and I began breaking down the equipment and carrying it to the guesthouse.

What happened next had been shoved into the crevices of the memory steam trunk. Going through memory baggage can be a quick task, but this is the part where it got difficult. These are the memories I had been piling layer upon layer into the steam trunk of my memories related to that season, yet I was trapped in a sports car with my second husband racing to a house I hadn't laid eyes on in years. My heart pounded in my ears and throat while tears raced down my face. I had finally reached the precipice of why I left.

I wore a burgundy dress that hit at my knees. The neckline didn't plunge very deep, but it was sleeveless, which made me very aware of the number of push-ups I had not completed in the last month. Peter arrived just as I finished putting on my lip-gloss and re-tousled my hair with product to keep the waves semi-uniform. His shirt was rumpled with a small patch of grease on his left side slightly above his belt. As soon as he entered the guesthouse, he began loosening his tie and taking off his shoes. I came down the stairs with my check list because a few lighting props needed to be returned to a photography friend that evening for a shoot she was doing the next day. Peter's jaw dropped and his cheeks flushed.

"You forgot didn't you," I shook my head and stopped in the middle of the stairs.

His brows arched and he pressed his lips together while nodding. I laughed. He moved toward me with arms outstretched.

"But you look so good I should take you out," he smiled.

I giggled as we hugged hello. "I believe you should. The reservations were made a month ago. If they did take out, I would go there in sweatpants and eat on the sofa here."

He laughed. "No no. You shouldn't change clothes. Are you ready?" He began to put his shoes back on his feet.

I looked at my lighting equipment in the living room and checked my clipboard. "I forgot to bring a light and light stand back that need to be returned to Karen tonight. Mind if I run go grab it?"

"I'll drive the car up and we can just meet in the driveway," he said while fussing with his shoe.

I noticed his shirt collar was flipped up in the back, which meant it had probably been that way all day since he lived alone. He also had what looked like a faded barbecue handprint on his right shoulder. He looked up at me and cocked his head to one side. "What?"

I laughed. "Oh honey, you are not fit for people. Was it a hard day?"

His entire countenance fell. He nodded like a small child tired of being brave on the playground with all the big kids. I walked over to him and climbed in his lap before kissing his cheek.

"We can always get reservations again. Let's just order pizza or something easy."

He nuzzled my cheek with his nose and smiled. "You are so New York. How about I fire the grill for some burgers or something easy?"

"You may need to go to the store. Per usual, I don't have food in my fridge."

He laughed, "Gaw, what kind of bachelorette are you!"

"The kind dating a man who can cook really well."

We kissed, and then he pushed me toward the door. "Go get your stuff while I make a grocery list."

I blew him a kiss as I slipped on my flip-flops, which were next to the front door. I practically bounced to the main house.

No one was supposed to be home. Seymour and his wife had arrived as Jenny and I were emptying the spare bedroom of equipment. Jenny and I shoved some boxes from the hallway back into the room once the equipment was removed.

The grandparents' arrival was unplanned, which typically meant going out to dinner at Puckett's or some other favorite dive of Seymour's. Jenny's mother had hurried me out the door for my date, which was why I forgot the light stand. I slipped back into the silent house thinking through my mental to do list for the exhibition.

I didn't see any purses or hear the typical noises of Jenny's grandmother bustling to clean (or re-clean as was often the case) the kitchen and dining room. Typically at that time of day if the grandparents were home, Seymour was asleep sitting up and snoring on the living room couch with his boots on the glass coffee table. Also, the typical noise was the television playing a 24/7 news station when they were in the main house. I looked around the living room, but the house was silent. Unusually, even the television was silent and gray on the wall above the fireplace mantle. *They must have gone to dinner*, I thought as I slipped down the emptied hallway toward the bedrooms.

I noticed the spare bedroom door was shut, but again, I thought, *Oh they must have closed off the mess before leaving.*

I neared the door with barely audible "flip flop, flip flop, flip flop" noises from my feet. With no one seeming to be home, I didn't think about it, but as my hand grabbed the crystal knob, I heard something and jumped at the sudden sound echoing in the *not-so-alone* house.

As I stretched my arm again and placed my hand on the knob, I told myself that a box must have shifted.

You know that catch in your stomach when you think someone might be in a room? When it's dark, your hand might slip through a crack and flip on the light switch to make sure you aren't entering in the dark and can see what monster might be lurking? Typically, you flip on the light to find a room devoid of monsters, but on the occasion you see someone in the room, you might turn into an eight second viral video on the internet, depending on the extremity of your reaction.

The catch in my stomach hit as I turned the knob. I opened the door very slowly and with a hyper-awareness that someone or something might be in the room. I didn't scream or run or shout. I froze.

I opened the door ever so slowly with a suddenly awareness that someone or something might be in the room. Seymour lay on the twin bed with one arm crooked behind his head and the other straight beside his body. His walnut face didn't flinch. Any normal person might sit up startled or blush in embarrassment, even if they were innocent. Seymour remained perfectly still. As I opened the door, I saw Jenny crouched over him but backing away with her hands clasped tightly together. She looked at me for a fleeting second and then looked away. I walked straight for the light box and stand, so my path directly bisected the room to the opposite corner.

Words began pouring out of my mouth, "I didn't realize anyone was home. I have to return this lighting equipment to my friend Karen who loaned it to me for the shoot today, and I just realized it was missing, so I walked over here and didn't realize anyone was home. Your wife told me that you had dinner reservations." The words meshed together as if they were one word, so when I stopped, Seymour chuckled slowly.

"The women-folk are taking care of that. I'm surprised you didn't knock."

I froze again. My stomach knotted. I suddenly felt very sick. I glanced at Jenny who was holding one elbow and looking pointedly away from me at the floor.

"I didn't knock because you weren't supposed to be here," I said slowly and turned to look at him while holding my light.

He lay so still in his denim and flannel and boots. As I turned, he moved the other arm to crook behind his head. He lay there without a pillow. The light stand had wheels that locked. I unlocked the light and moved it across the room rather than attempt to collapse it.

"Well maybe next time you see a door closed you'll knock to see if someone is in there," he said quietly.

My throat squeezed shut. I looked him straight in the face. His eyes were open yet slightly squinting as he stared straight at me. His mouth slightly frowned as his lips pursed. I opened and shut my mouth. My eyes followed his mouth down the length of his body because his booted feet were the closest part of his person to the open door of the spare room. His pants were unzipped.

"Jenny, I need your help moving some equipment," I said without looking at him.

She was silent.

"Jenny can help you when she's finished in here."

She didn't move. I stood between them in my return diagonal across the room back to the door. I kept my eyes on the door and took a deep breath. "I believe she's finished being in here sir."

He sat up and leaned on one elbow so quickly that I took a step away from him. I half ducked expecting to be hit or an object to fly my direction.

"She still has some boxes to move for her mother in here, so I'll continue managing her progress on what she needs to do in this room."

I looked at Jenny. "Hey, are you okay in here? I could use your help and you can finish whatever your mom needs in a few minutes?"

She looked up at me, but I didn't recognize her face. She was drained of all color. She nodded.

Seymour lay back in his former position on the bed and said, "See. She's fine. Why don't you call your man have him come help you move your stuff?"

The hairs on the back of my neck stood up. I spun around so quickly that he flinched this time. "My what?"

T he smile on his face spread slowly. "I thought you were from the South dahlin'. I didn't mean to offend."

I smiled. "I'm not offended in the least, darlin'." I turned and looked at Jenny. "I'll be right outside if you need anything."

She nodded and looked back at the floor with both arms crossed in front of her.

"You best run along now and not miss your date," Seymour said slightly louder than normal.

"And you best zip your fly before you have an accident," I said sharply.

He was laying again on the twin bed with his arms crooked behind his head to serve as a pillow. We looked one another in the eye. "Naw. There won't be an accident." Then he mouthed, "No proof."

My jaw dropped as though he threw a boulder in my gut. His smile spread across his wrinkled face. I continued my walk out the door with the light stand rolling beside me. I paused as I entered the hallway.

"I'll be back in a few minutes to collect the rest," I found myself saying. My voice seemed disconnected.

"Sounds fine," Seymour said and then softly "Jenny."

I hurried to the kitchen. I could hear what might have been women talking. My palms were dripping with sweat. My stomach turned. *Had that really happened? Did I just leave her there to...? Surely not...*

I entered the kitchen with both women standing by the stove. A pile of bags from a grocery and take-out run sat on the counter. I began to speak. They turned at looked at me so slowly. I realized all at once that I lived in the *guest*house. It dawned on me that the mountains of laundry I moved and the emotional baggage I had organized with and for them were things a helper did. They weren't doing life with me. They were doing life parallel to me, and that reality became even more apparent as I shared what I had experienced.

Neither woman's expression changed. They stood almost like bookends to the stove. Their faces, hair, and even physical stance of one hand on a hip and the other bracing against the counter made them look like twins, yet they were decidedly two different ages of the same person form.

I finished with how he mouthed "No proof" and said, "So, what should we do?"

I held the still not collapsed light stand and light. The cord was looped in my hand as I gripped the stem of the light stand. I stood straight with my flip-flopped feet planted firmly and my shoulders squared. Their eyes seemed to stare through my red dress and their voices seemed distant as though not their own.

One of them said, "Well you could have misunderstood him if he mouthed something."

The other said, "I'm not exactly sure what you are insinuating. Maybe you are mistaken."

They looked to one another and spoke without diverting their gaze from each other. I almost couldn't tell who was speaking because the exchange overlapped so seamlessly, "Yes. You must be mistaken. That sounds like too odd of an exchange to worry your head about tonight while your man is waiting. Why don't you hurry on out to your date?"

My body turned to a burning torch. My cheeks were red. I wasn't crying but my eyes burned. They continued nodding at each other and not looking at me. I simply nodded and backed out of the kitchen. I left the light in the foyer and hurried down the hallway.

I swung open the door without knocking and straight lied, "Jenny, your grandmother needs you in the kitchen."

She was sitting on the bed next to Seymour with her feet on the floor. She looked at me with wide eyes.

"Yeah?"

"Yeah hurry up. Dinner's almost ready."

Seymour frowned at me and motioned with his hand for Jenny to come to him, "Give me a kiss before you help your grandmother."

She kissed his cheek super fast and he smacked her bottom as she moved away from him. She winced but raced out of the room.

I heard her little voice asking in the kitchen how she could help with dinner while I slipped out the front door with the light stand and light in my hand as though I was rolling a torch. Dusk had fallen and faded into evening. I rolled the light down the driveway feeling as though I was on fire. The thought to actually collapse the light stand never entered my mind. I could hear a car engine and almost ran into Peter's car as he inched up the driveway.

His headlights filled my view. I couldn't even see his car. I stopped like a deer in the road and shook my head. I heard the parking brake engage. His door slammed and he grabbed my shoulders. I think he was speaking (shouting?).

"I think what just happened wasn't okay but there's no proof Peter. I just...there's no proof. What do I do with no proof? I just found them and the light and I found and no proof Peter no proof," I babbled with the images replaying over and over in my head.

"Hey, look at me. What happened?"

Now, this might sound a bit crazy, but in spite of this circumstance that I found myself in, everything stopped as I looked into those eyes. In a crystal clear knowing in my gut, I knew that instant that I was going to marry that man. Calm, radiant peace wrapped around me so completely that I felt like I had found home. I began to cry. I had no words left. He held me in the middle of the driveway until I could talk. He then guided me to the trunk of the car to collapse the light stand.

Once we left the driveway and Peter was driving, I began to tell him everything from beginning to end. He held my hand the whole way to Karen's house. As we pulled into her driveway, I finished the story. I could barely keep myself together and said between fresh tears and snot, "I just don't know what to do."

My whole body shook while my hands held my face between my knees.

Peter killed the engine before turning in his seat. He touched my shoulder and I sat up. He grabbed both of my hands and spoke as though he was measuring each phrase, "What you are suggesting...what you saw... I believe you."

The ugly crying began, so I simply nodded. He cupped my chin and turned my face up to his. "But Anni, he's right. There is no proof."

I felt vomit churning in my gut, but then he said the words that changed everything: "But if you are right like I believe you are, one day, there will be proof, so we will protect that little girl as long as we possibly can, and we will do whatever we can until there is proof or she can move out on her own to protect herself."

Inhaling:
air resembling honey
fresh
from the hive
sultry
sticky
pulsing with
life and
death,
food and
feces

Breathing:
air thrusting lungs
thick
like water
burning
aching
drenched with
tears and
gasps,
anger and
sadness

Gasping:
air confronting face
hot
with spit
short
fast
exploding with

life

and

gasps,

feces

and

sadness

-Jenny, age 15, poetry diary

Jenny

I couldn't see their faces.

    Suddenly I realized that the wet on my face was coming from my own eyes. One man knelt a few feet away from me and held his badge toward me. A sound came deep from my core. The other remained standing and was talking into a walkie-talkie on his shoulder. Their uniforms were black.
    I took the badge and asked him to recite his badge number and precinct number. His voice remained steady and calm. He repeated his name as Bryan and how Peter called them and how I was safe.
    "Peter?"
    "Yes, Peter and Anni. They are here, but because there is blood, we have to process everything and get your statement and make sure you are okay. When we get the okay, you can see them. Do you feel safe now because you are safe."
    I held his badge to my chest and cried. "Are you sure I'm really safe?"
    His words disappeared as I closed my eyes. I could hear Seymour whispering in my ear like he did when I was a kid, and I was still afraid. My whole body shook. I could hear him saying, "No one can find out. This is our secret. Our special secret."

Everything disappeared.

DUSK WITH AN EMPTY
STEAM TRUNK OF MEMORIES
ANNI

We let them in the front door with the key, but our friend and police officer Bryan told us not to follow. The ambulance sirens burned my eardrums. The crime scene investigators wouldn't let me touch her. I heard someone say she passed out from shock.

Peter had to hold me back in the street while they processed the scene and took her statement. Bryan stood between the ambulance and us. His gentle baritone quietly explained the next steps to Peter and I before he took our statements. Peter gripped my waist and held my elbow the entire time. Every time a person entered or exited the mahogany colored front door I looked up and began to take a step toward the house. Peter would tug and me, and I would relax.

Their front lawn became a sea of people and tape and the swish of starched uniforms. Bryan advised we say nothing before he went to check with his commanding officer on protocol related to us. Neighbors appeared. A few approached us with the concerned questions. They were especially alarmed since it had been almost two years since Peter or I had set foot in the neighborhood. Peter softly told everyone to go home and that we were assured everything would be fine soon. (I wasn't certain if he was lying or speaking what we hoped would be the outcome). Only a few of them recognized Peter, and the few who recognized me attempted small talk with me. Apparently, I didn't even acknowledge their presence. Peter told me later that they called me "rude" as they were walking away from me. I was simply watching and waiting in the street for that little girl.

    When she was escorted out the door, I gasped. Gone were the awkwardly long arms and legs of childhood. Her hair flowed down her back, but her stance was slouched beneath a blanket wrapped around her shoulders. I think I called her name because she looked at me. No one stopped her from running to our arms. I took a few steps into the grass. We sank in the lawn with Peter's arms around us.

    "Can I go home with you?" her little voice, so matured in the time since I had seen her, still sounded like the little girl I saw on the guesthouse welcome mat my first day.

    "I don't know. I hope so," I couldn't lie.

    She nodded. "But now there's proof, right?"

    All the air left my lungs. Her round, bloodshot eyes burned into mine. I heard Peter gasp, but everything seemed to stop.

    Like it did in the car, the memory of Seymour mouthing those words shot passed my eyes. How quickly I forgot she was in the room. How quickly I forgot she probably saw the same thing, and for a split second, I kicked myself for never asking her.

    I had tried to get her school counselor involved. I took meetings with lawyer friends.

Unfortunately with Jenny being a minor, I was in a corner if she didn't offer the information unprompted. In the eyes of the judicial system, I would look like a manipulator, which could ruin her, my career, my reputation, and much more.

Honestly, Seymour's reach, even after retirement from the legal system, terrified me, so I didn't press forward as much as I had originally wanted to push. Now, here I was staring at two big puddles of eyes after her mouth said, "But now there's proof, right?"

In the seconds after all this flashed before my eyes and Jenny asked the question, we both looked at Peter. I asked him so softly, "Seymour couldn't bury real evidence, could he?"

He hugged us into his chest. I felt tears hit the top of my head. The three of us leaned together and simply cried. Time began again when Bryan took a knee next to Peter and explained that Jenny needed to be escorted separately from us. She squeezed us both tighter and buried her face into Peter's chest.

"You can trust Bryan, okay?" he said, but he didn't loosen his grip.

She began to nod and break the embrace. We brushed the grass off our knees and all straightened to standing. Bryan told us that we had to make sure that everything was above reproach and promised Jenny that she was in the best of hands with his precinct.

My heart burst with gratitude when he looked at her and said, "We believe you. It is our job to protect you, and we will. I give you my word." She squared her shoulders, took a deep breath, and nodded. They walked away from us, and I felt as though I could breathe again.

Bryan knew the story. We had approached him all those years ago, but he said even then that his hands were tied. Today, he gave his word as a protector, and I knew that no matter where she went, he would ensure Seymour never touched her again.

Peter and I followed her to the police department a few miles away from the house. Peter had the clarity of though to call our attorney on the drive. When we arrived to the precinct, the hum of the drink machine and keyboards clicking filled the air. We sat on wooden chairs in a small waiting area while waiting for them to finish their protocol with Jenny. Peter was able to secure us some surprisingly good coffee as we shifted uncomfortably.

"Remember the barbecue I catered?" his voice, though whispered, seemed to slice the air.

"Barbecue?" I almost choked on my coffee.

"Sorry," he moved to help but I shook my head at him. He continued, "That barbecue that was Jenny's dad's birthday."

I looked at him wide eyed. "I had completely forgotten you got your restaurant to do that dinner…huh…I remember he arrived home in the middle of the night, so in the course of maybe 36 or 48 hours, Jenny's mother and grandmother put on this ridiculously huge 'Barbecue Birthday Bash' or something like that."

He nodded and sipped his coffee. "Yeah. Well, do you remember how Duncan pulled me aside during set up?"

My eyes scrunched and I shook my head with a frown. The only image in my head from setting up for the party was lounging in yellow and white lawn chairs with lemonade and Jenny. We had grabbed mint from the garden to crush into our lemonade, dawned oversized "movie star" sunglasses, and directed the rental company on where to put the tables and chairs. Her giggle kept the set up team laughing and playing along with our game.

Peter broke my thoughts, "Yeah. So, um, that night Duncan and I were talking because he was trying to find out who actually was invited to the thing. Apparently he had no say in the matter and really had hoped to disappear with his wife for his birthday. It's funny. I remember that day so clearly because it's the most Duncan and I ever talked since he was out on assignment so much when you lived there, ya know?"

"Yeah. He has to handle some significant government cases."

"I gathered," Peter paused to sip his coffee again and continued. "Anyway, he never referred to Seymour by name when we talked. It's still odd to think about it now. Duncan asked me if you or I knew if 'he' was coming and if someone was monitoring drinks. I mean, I thought it was so strange at the time. You'd been there long enough, so it might have made sense to you, but all I knew was that my team had dispensers for lemonade and tea and the family had ice buckets for longnecks on the deck outside. Duncan turned so red, Anni. I think you were down on the lawn, but I gotta tell you, he was angry that 'he' was coming and there was going to be alcohol. I offered for him to grab a beer and hide the rest if he thought it would be an issue for Seymour. Duncan said something that stuck with me that night, 'It might be my only option. That man is no good with alcohol. He's really not good at all.'"

"Duncan said that Seymour wasn't good at all?"

Peter nodded. We both turned our gazes to the wall opposite our chairs. We continued silently sipping our coffees side by side.

I lost myself in the memory of that night during our silence. I remembered that night quite clearly because Seymour did get drunk and his wife laughed, waving people off of him like it was a big joke. She did manage to get him to lie down on the pullout sofa in the office with a trashcan by his head.

I specifically remembered the trashcan the next day because Duncan made an appointment with me during his party to come to his home office. The trashcan didn't have a liner in it and was in the middle of the room. I thought it was odd until I noticed the impressions of where the pullout mattress had been all night. I sat on the reassembled sofa to sign a hefty document related to guardianship when he was out of town. I looked at Duncan like he was crazy, but I didn't dare say anything in front of the notary and lawyer he had seated in the room.

Originally, what clicked in my mind about the document was that I hadn't realized how bad his wife's depression was sinking because this was before the suicide attempt and hospital stay.

When I asked him if that's why he felt the guardianship was necessary, he filled me in on some of his concerns about her and that "her parents aren't exactly the ideal caretakers, given their ages and responsibilities at the farm."

Thinking back with the new information Peter had shared, I began wondering what Duncan knew then that he had no proof to address.

Bryan appeared, which broke my thoughts. He introduced us to some investigators who had to work this case. They pulled us into a conference room for privacy before we spoke any further.

The investigators made it clear that this was suspected child abuse and that Jenny's part in the story was self-defense. At that point, we were on their same page despite not really knowing what had actually happened prior to receiving the phone call from Jenny. We assured the investigators that we were prepared for whatever needed to be shared.

I needed to run to the restroom, so when I came back, the female investigator pulled me into a separate room from Peter. Suddenly my coffee didn't taste as good.

The concentration of the interview was that it seemed surprising that there had been little to no contact in at least two years, if not longer. The officer walked me back through my testimony with questions under the guise that it was a final "read it, write it, and sign it kind of thing."

After thirty minutes of scrutinizing, I realized what was happening. I should have shut my mouth and waited for my attorney. I should have said I wouldn't say anything without my husband present. I should have done a list of things, but instead, I began to speak very quietly while tears cascaded down my face.

"Look. I'm tired of this. Let's just cut to the chase. What would you do if you got this phone call? Would you say, 'Sorry honey, but we haven't talked in years. How do I know you aren't lying? I don't know you," I wiped snot on my sleeve and tried to take a breath only to feel my heart pounding in my ears. The next words came out in a weeping rage, "No you don't do that because you stood in that kitchen and watched the faces of the two women whose job it is to protect her--you watched their faces carry almost no expression before turning to denial. You tromped through that house and guesthouse--always aware that you weren't family, and their denial blocked you from doing anything. You saw in that little girl's eyes the relief when you appeared--like she was drinking life--and you kept that key that mysteriously appeared in the mail--praying you'd never have to use it. Literally praying. I can't tell you how many church services I have sat through and midnights in the dark and showers alone where I have prayed and prayed and prayed that I was wrong, but I kept that blasted key because when I did get the call, my heart told me to find that key. It wasn't ever a mystery, but now, I had a reason. Now there would be proof without heresy, so I answered that phone and dang it--excuse me--I marched straight into Hell with all my armor on because I FINALLY had the opportunity to set loose the truth and free the one person who did nothing to ask for this life. I held it in my heart for years the truth--mulling it over--praying it through--wondering if leaving was the worst decision I could have ever made, but as horrible as today is, I finally have peace because that little girl is finally safe. She is finally free, and I got to help make that happen. So don't look at me with doubtful eyes and ask stupid questions that you know in your gut are only for protocol and rhetoric. You know you believe me because you would have done the same thing in my shoes, and if you wouldn't, God save you and this entire unit from cowardice. I tried to make my stand years ago, but I had no undeniable proof because an old man lied to a little girl despite what I had seen. I'm making my stand today. If you don't keep that child safe and at least send her to her aunt's house in Maine, then justice is not a work. So help me, I'll drive her myself because it is the right thing to do. We both know it is, so don't look at me with doubt. Be grateful someone showed up, called you, and put a win your pocket over child abuse, rape, and molestation. I am taking my stand today. I took my stand, so either continue questioning because you don't understand how I fit into this story--or take my word for it--because I am telling you the truth."

    I ugly-cried the entire way through and a loud sob erupted from my core at the end. The police officer, Maya, sat quietly while I pushed back my chair and stood to show I was literally drawing the line and taking a stand. As I quaked with tears, I saw her sweet face was streaked with tears as well.

    Her voice came out like honey but softer. "You're right. It is protocol. It's just hard to believe that you knew all this time, tried to fight it, and that child's own mother never believed you," she shook her head.

    "Denial is far too powerful in this family ma'am," I replied, barely above a whisper.

Her tone matched mine as she stated, "It was in mine, too."

We looked at one another across the conference table. She sat. I stood. Our eyes locked. Quickly, I sank to my chair and placed my hands on her hands that were holding a trembling pen over a yellow legal pad. Without thinking, I looked her steadily in the eye, "Then for the trauma where no one seemed to find you or want to rescue you, my stand is for you to be found, too."

The officer began to weep. I moved around the table, unable to contain myself. We embraced like sisters and wept. A knock on the conference room door startled us as her partner reentered.

"Is everything okay? Your husband is wrapped up and waiting for you," he hovered in the open door.

Maya nodded and wiped her face free of tears. "We were finished. I need to wrap up my notes, but we're good here. Unless you have anything to add, ma'am?"

I grabbed my purse from the floor next to my chair and began to fumble around in it. I held up a finger and said, "Look. I don't know how things work. I don't know if you are building a case or what. He is a former politician. I think he was a judge, and he knows people. He knows how to keep things quiet, but you need evidence." I pulled out the note and house key. "I received these a couple years ago. It may not be anything, but it's how I knew I could get into the house." I took a deep breath before setting them on the table. "We've already gone through my background, but there aren't any pictures for evidence. I do, however, keep a detailed journal. These are from when I lived there. Everything I shared can be found by date. If you think they'll help, I have nothing to hide. Also, Duncan had a nanny cam or some kind of video surveillance at the house that he didn't tell anyone but me about, so I don't know when it was installed. He told me gave me permission that in an emergency, I'd know who I was to tell about it. If you can get those records, they should line up with what I wrote. Here's the business card he gave me for that."

Wide-eyed, the officers looked at me when I handed them the journal and the card from my purse. "We'll take them for processing. They may prove useless since it's all circumstantial at this point, but we appreciate your cooperation."

I looked at my now empty hands. My palms seemed unusually white. Ever so quietly, I mustered the courage to say, "I've never had proof until today, and even then, it could melt into a curtain of denial like it did the first time."

Maya, the female officer, touch my arm and said, "But you're trying, and that will give her hope and a future of goodness."

I nodded with more tears splashing my hands. "May we stay until her aunt or father arrive?"

They exchanged looks. Maya's partner said, "Actually, I thought you knew. The family lawyer is already here and has requested that you stay until temporary custody is decided by the State."

I felt the color drain from my entire body. "Duncan isn't here?"

"No ma'am."

"Do you know why?"

"All we can tell you is that the delicacy and nature of his job are---"

I finished, "Vital to national security. I know I guess I thought he'd show up. He's kind of the white knight like that for our country."

The officers exchanged smiles revealing that they understood my meaning, probably better than I did. Peter appeared at the door with an imposingly large man in a gray suit and blue and red striped tie.

"Anni, Duncan's attorney and the social worker would like to have a word with us," his brows arched and he glanced up and down at the man to indicate the enormity of the man.

At least 6'7", he was at least a head taller than Peter and twice as thick in the chest. I had a feeling he could bench-press all of us without sweating. I had a fleeting thought of wonder if he was really an attorney.

"May we use your conference room?" he asked. His soft voice boomed and echoed in the gray-green room.

"Certainly," the officers motioned to the table and scurried out of the room.

Peter sat beside me and held my hand. I shook as though chilled.

"In the event of Duncan _____'s absence and a question of custody should arise in the case of Jenny, he has requested that the two of you be granted a temporary guardianship."

I sputtered, "But I thought that was just when I was living there since his wife was so ill and then she had to go out west for treatment and---"

The attorney shook his head and held up a hand. "No. These documents indicate that until she is 18 that this guardianship would go into effect, but upon that date, she would be left to her own authority and the living situation of her choosing."

The social worker interjected. I had barely noticed her appearance in her brown power suit and brown shoes, "This is a highly unusual matter, but due to Jenny's father's position in the government, you have already been approved as fit temporary guardianship until he returns stateside. It has been stressed to us that you have the security clearance and background check necessary."

Peter told me later that they began explaining the legal precedence, how we could refuse, and all the other details he made them clarify. Since we married after the original document was signed, he was concerned how it could be argued in court, but apparently they had documentation related to that, which we needed to sign. The lights in the room grew hot and I began to see stars. I put my head between my knees and breathed deeply. Peter patted my back and I slowly sat up. "It's like Duncan knew this day could come."

Peter did a double take and held up at hand at the attorney and social worker. "Pardon me, but I think we need a moment. Water or sprite or something would be helpful too please."

Apparently I had turned a white-green color. He held my hands and asked me to repeat myself, which I did. His brows furrowed together, and his mouth frowned. Then he leaned and whispered in my ear, "They don't really have family, and you know he never trusted Seymour. We don't really know why, but remember that birthday barbecue? He hid the alcohol because he didn't want to see or deal with a drunk Seymour and he told me that night that he felt better when he knew I was going to be around the house and Seymour when he had to go out of town."

I nodded and whispered back to him, "I remember you mentioning how relieved he was that you had been around more. Peter, it's just so surreal. I never actually believed we'd have guardianship. I just thought she might get to visit. I didn't realize all that old paperwork still applied."

He squeezed my hands and said in a normal voice, "It's okay. Let's take her away from this place as soon as they let her go. Pizza and ice cream like we used to on Fridays?"

I could feel my mouth trembling and eyes burning with more tears. I think I nodded because the attorney and social worker reappeared with water and Sprite. We agreed to sign the papers. Our attorney was escorted in and read over the paperwork as well. With fresh blue ink, we signed guardianship and met Jenny in the hallway.

FOUND

GRANDMOTHER

"Disgraceful. Absolutely disgraceful," I could hear him clucking behind me. "Women of a certain age should never wear color. They are to be the matriarchs and pillars of their families, not ridiculous roses or orchids or mums in bloom at a party."

I myself was wearing a deep green dress similar to the sapphire one he had complimented his best friend's wife on wearing the day prior at a business luncheon for the firm. I made no comment. It was the last day I wore that dress. All women were wearing reds and pinks and greens that day. Actually, it might have been the last time I wore a dress in any color other than black, gray, or brown. I was 24.

That memory came to me often when I stood in front of my closet doors. My closet had a "classic" theme to it. At least, that's how I described it to my friends. I didn't tell them about the early alcoholic rages in our marriage, so I chose long sleeves and long skirts to cover bruises better. His rage eased after Daughter was born, but it never quite disappeared. Even though he was as an alcoholic wife beater, leaving him would have been a disgrace for both of us, so I stayed.

Returning to the house to see police tape and evidence tags, my world hazed suddenly into focus. Gone were the stories of the Old South ways and sending everyone into the woods with their heads filled with faeries and fantasies to drown out the shadows and screams. Gone was the ability to make anything Seymour said seem positive or with love toward me, my children, or grandchildren. I remember firing our gardener when he tried to tell me that something else could be happening, but that yellow tape across the driveway and door wide open at Daughter and Duncan's house…

    I drove Seymour back to the farm and we brought Daughter with us. She had fallen asleep in the car, so she missed the police tape. We circled the street without speaking to a soul. He paled at the sight of the marked police cruiser sitting in front of the house. He remarked, "With all this activity, we may want to head on home, don't you think?"

    The police interviewed him in the hospital, but somehow, he told them that he would show up to the precinct for an appointment the next day rather than give a statement about the situation. Daughter and I missed the discussion, so I only knew what Seymour recounted as we entered the room. I can only imagine what actually happened. He stayed a lawyer, judge, and politician for a long time without even a blip on his reputation.

    When we arrived to the house, Seymour suggested I change clothes and loan Daughter some pajamas for the evening. I clenched my fists, tucked him into bed, and smelled the remnants of whiskey on his breath and clothes.

    There's only so long you can live with denial. Eventually you have a breaking point because you know the denial is a sickness. You know you weren't always this way… So, you stand, alone in your room, staring at the closet, and you decide that if you really hate the clothes he's told you to wear or not--for yourself. And you spy that green dress in a back corner of your closet from when you were 16 that you wore to Union Station when your father took you for a grown up lunch away from your mother. And you remember the dreams, the hopes, the voice you carried...was it really that long ago?

    I asked myself aloud, "Was I really this person in brown with wrinkles and dyed hair and painted on eyebrows?"

    I knew I had to decide who I was, even if I didn't know right that moment, and eventually I was going to have to take the reigns or continue denying that I could live my own life.

    I looked at that green dress and pulled it off the closet hook. Green had been my signature color from childhood until marriage. I would have worn it as my wedding dress color if Seymour hadn't insisted on buying me a white dress.

    Holding that dress, our entire marriage flashed before my eyes and landed in crumpled bits and pieces of the last few questionable years.

    "Dahlin' would you bring me somethin' to drink. I am so parched from that hospital air," he called from the bed.

    I put the green dress back in the closet and squared my shoulders. I felt very awake and very alert with a new idea forming deep within my person. "Oh certainly I'll bring you a drink."

FOUND

Jenny's Mother (aka Daughter)

Dark.
No alarm.
No light from windows.
Warm with sheets and comforters.
But an empty house.
Such an empty house.
Tears. Felt the tears coming.
Ran to the bathroom, but stumbled as though hadn't walked in days.
Had it been days?
Fumbled to the sink to splash water on face but saw these hands. Two beautiful white hands with freckles and the remnants of a manicure. They seemed old and young at once with pink color but paper-thin skin.
Splashed the face with sink water.
Looked up in the mirror and backed away from the counter.
Freckles from summer days riding the horse mistakenly not mine.
Summer days at the pool and beachside with a bikini on a perfectly curved body.
Blinked once.
Blinked twice.
Squeezed eyes shut.
Opened.

Same oval face with bright eyes and lips parting almost in an "o."
Hands touched cheeks.
Real.
Solid.
Fingers dragged through bottle-bleached highlights that somehow look as young and fresh as the first day of summer.
Real?
Blinked again.
And again.
Tears cascaded down the flawlessly freckled face. Rivers of mascara washed foundation powder and red blush to the face's throat.
Noticed the hands again.
Little bones moving with angelic precision.
Wrists devoid of watches, bracelets or adornments.
Only a wedding band.
A ringing shattered the quiet in the distance.
Hands wiped face clean.
This face...this beautiful face...
Fumbled in the drawer through bottles, piling them on the counter, and pulling out a daily pill organizer.
Filled. All were still there.
Solid counter.
Solid pills.
Solid sound of water plummeting in the sink.
Dumped each bottle and counted them before checking the calendar on the counter.
Looked back to the mirror.
Same face.
Not an overdose.
Not a hallucination.

Each wipe of tears removed another layer of make-up to reveal fresher skin.
"She'll have to call you back," came a familiar voice behind...a female voice from long ago too.
Not an overdose. "7, 8, 9"
Not a hallucination. "2, 3, 4"
"Are you okay?"
Shook head side to side.
Gray-green eyes opened wider at reflection, seeing person come into view.
Turned to face her.
"Anni, do you see what I see?"
"What do you see?"
Tears fell harder.
Sobs erupted into choking and tears and loud cries.
Arms encircled.
She placed a phone on the bathroom counter and a duffel bag on the floor.
The air filled with words swirling around us with golden rays of light.
Nothing spoken to answer the question yet.
"That's your reflection."
The words floated between us and sank deep.
Stepped back once.
Twice.
Naked eyelids shut over shining eyes.
Turned to face mirror again.
Eyes opened slowly to see reflection.
Stood taller.
Shaking hands straightened hair behind ears.
Looked up and down the length of the whole reflection.
"It is me?"
Warm hand placed on shoulder from Anni.

FOUND

We linger amid the unspoken words and memories that hovered in the atmosphere. Our eyes take in the reflections in the mirror with that terrible bathroom lighting.
"Take her home. She's free."
Embraced for a moment.
Tears.
Slide back into sheets.
Warm.
Dark.
Disappear.

A Time Later
Anni

With the radio silenced, we listened to the crunch of gravel, hush of the country lanes with their worn asphalt, whine of pot-holed city streets under construction, and hum of the newly laid interstate asphalt. I checked her reflection in the rearview mirror, but she simply stared out the window or at her hands. We didn't speak, and I questioned our decision in even going to the house at all.

As we pulled into the neighborhood, the street screeched in my ears. I heard her shift and straighten. We locked eyes for the first time in the rearview mirror. Her hair tumbled to her elbows over a gray linen dress as she crossed her arms. Neither of us had the will to smile.

A black Town Car pulled out of the driveway and hurried down the street passed us. I parked the car on the curb. The sun was fading behind the house. I identified a single lamplight burning in the front left room. I turned off the car and got out, yet I stood transfixed with the car door open. My eyes soaked in every brick, every tree, and every blade of grass.

Our last time to be here the crime tape was falling and tracks of people trudging through the yard were still evident. The shrubs looked recently trimmed, and the planters held dark mulch against fresh green sod. The brick and ivy-covered mailbox looked freshly pruned and possibly painted.

After an eternity of staring, I opened the back door for her, but she didn't move. She stared out the door. I bent down to look at her, but her face was soaked. Even looking at me, I doubt she could have seen more than the watery lens of tears morphing reality into swirling paint strokes. Before I could speak, Peter turned in his seat to look at her. I had almost forgotten he chose to ride with us.

"This is as far as you have to go. You asked to see them, and if this is enough for you, then we'll start the car and go straight home," he said.

She nodded and wiped her faced with a single hand. She didn't speak.

Peter continued, staring straight at her face, "We supported you in not attending the funeral today. We supported you in not going to the graveside service today. We will support you in not crossing that threshold for the rest of your life, if that's what you want, but if you want to go in, you will not be going alone. Seymour may be dead, but we're still not letting you in that place alone today or ever."

She jumped at the word 'dead' being spoken so boldly, without condolence or false positivity. Her eyes flew to his. I watched his gaze hold onto hers in a way only a daddy can look at a daughter. She nodded, bottom lip trembling, and her hand reached for the door handle.

I straightened and stared at the house again. I saw shadows moving and heard voices talking, but their words were muffled through the metal and glass. Jenny stepped out of the car and squeezed my hand before silently walking to the mailbox. She smoothed out a crumpled envelope and placed it inside the mailbox. Peter stepped outside the car as well. She nodded at each of us, took a deep breath, and walked back to the car. He and I looked at each other across the roof. I looked at the door of the house for myself again.

After we broke the news of Seymour's heart attack and sudden death, we braced ourselves for all sorts of reactions. She sat quietly at first with no expression whatsoever. She asked a few questions about the funeral and if her mother or grandmother were the ones who called us. Peter explained that it was actually Mr. Hobbes who contacted us because Duncan had ensured that all contact was severed with them during and after the police investigation. Peter quietly assured her, "Mr. Hobbes is a good gatekeeper for helping us keep you safe." At the word 'safe,' a single tear streaked her face. Then followed another and another. I held her and rocked as she soaked my shoulder while we curled up in her bed. Peter sat next to us with his arm around me. She eventually fell asleep as the crying subsided, so we decided to allow her to sleep on the decision to even attend any of the funeral related events.

Frankly, I was relieved when she chose not to attend Seymour's funeral. "He's gone and that's all I need to know. I forgave him, but it's not in me to celebrate his life or death," she told us the next morning, but she had added, "I do think it might be good to check on my mother and grandmother after the wake." With that statement, it was easy to believe we were going for her. We even contacted her dad who was in DC to get his opinion. He and Jenny's counselor agreed this could work in favor of her healing more. Of course, all these days and conversations related to Jenny and consumed my mind with what to do for her.

Standing there, looking at that front door, I realized how much I longed to see her mother and grandmother without Seymour pulling his puppet strings on them. I wanted to hear their voices without his shouting over them for his stories and his demands. Then, ever so quickly, the thought slipped in that I wanted to look in their eyes one more time as Jenny's guardian and her actual protector.

I took a deep breath and patted the car roof. My eyes scanned through the trees and fell back to Peter's furrowed brows and deep eyes. I smiled as tears trickled down my face, "She's safe. We found her in the knick of time." He reached across the roof to hold my hand. I realized that he was crying too. "Let me take my girls home." We squeezed hands before he took the driver seat and I moved to the front passenger seat.

He started the car and turned on the radio. Jenny and I groaned at the station he chose. He groaned back at us. "Don't make me listen to your music," he slid a wink at me while changing the station. Jenny chuckled, "Whatever. You know the baby can't stand your music." I laughed and rubbed my tummy, "No she doesn't. You're totally outnumbered." He smiled as he put the car in drive. "Well, what else can I do for my ladies? Ice cream and pizza?" Jenny and I squealed, "Yes!" I turned to look at her, and we both laughed. It felt good to release that gush of emotions as loud guffaws instead having them wreck us with sobs.

We left the neighborhood for the last time and quieted our giggles. Jenny sighed her giggle into a deep breath. She pressed her forehead against the glass and waved at a former neighbor bringing his trash to the end of his driveway. "I gave them the poem with my letter," she said matter-of-factly.

I nodded. "That's a bold move."

"I'm trying to convince myself not to turn around and grab it out of the mailbox."

"I wouldn't worry."

"Yeah. It's really over now isn't it?"

"Yes," Peter and I both answered her.

She took a deep breath and sank back into her seat. Her eyes shut, and she seemed to fall back to the age when I met her. "He's gone. It's over," she whispered and repeated. "He's gone. It's over…He's gone. It's over…"

A Funeral

Two women stood on the back porch of 1242 Vine Road. The sun had slipped through the trees, but its rays had not quite disappeared enough for stars to erupt through the navy and black evening blanket that pressed the sun into bed. The women stared at the horizon, barely noticing the slam of car doors coming from the front of the house. The catering staff had already cleared the back porch of signs of the dozens who attended the wake. Ignoring the staff's existence in the kitchen, the older woman stood with a glass of brandy while her daughter held the same glass of untouched white wine from hours earlier.

"The funeral was tasteful, don't you think?" the older woman asked while sipping her brandy. She didn't wait for the younger woman to respond. "I think it went well, and everyone seemed appropriately mournful about the unexpected heart attack."

"Beulah, hon, we're finished in the kitchen. I packed the leftovers in the fridge. Y'all will have enough food on top of the casseroles already packed in the freezer," the caterer appeared beside the older woman and hugged her.

"Thank you Genevieve. I'll see you at Bridge soon," she smiled and nodded.

The caterer slipped quietly back into the house. As the door shut, the last of the sun's rays disappeared. The house lights stretched down the lawn through the windowpane forms.

Beulah straightened and brushed an invisible hair from across her face before sipping more brandy. "We're free of him now. I finally got us free of him."

For the first time in weeks, Beulah and her daughter looked each other in the eyes. Without a word they nodded to each other and toasted. The daughter took a drink of her wine while Beulah finished her brandy in two deep swigs with her eyes shut. She gracefully set the glass on the porch railing with one hand while the other absently touched the cheerful emerald brooch. The mourners who mentioned it said, "What a lovely piece to remember Seymour by--you'll have to tell me the story of how and why he gave it to you." (Those are the kinds of things people say to Southern widows). Beulah genteelly replied to each of them, "Oh there's no story, but thank you for noticing my brooch." Her daughter took another sip of wine before seeming to fade into Beulah's shadow as night overtook middle Tennessee.

Beulah's voice rang across the back yard again as she stared at the rose covered guest cottage, "I finally got us rid of him."

FOUND

AUTHOR'S NOTE

While the characters and circumstances of this novel are fiction, the reality is that many families and individual persons have experienced one or many of the situations fictitiously portrayed in this novel.

If you are someone who experienced one or many of these circumstances but were not helped in your time of need, please know that you are not alone and there are many organizations willing to help you learn how to heal. Please don't hesitate to reach out and get the help* you need.

If you suspect someone is currently in an abusive situation, please contact the police* if there is an immediate danger as well as your local Department of Family and Children Services*, particularly if this person is a minor.

While the story and outcome are not typical for every situation and person, k**now that there are trained and equipped people who desire to help you.**

Note: *Domestic violence and all types of abuse are serious crimes and traumas. These situations often require considerable counseling to the persons victimized as well as the abuser.* ***Do not take matters for exacting punishment on an abuser into your own hands, and do not attempt to heal from abuse without seeking a certified counselor, psychologist, or psychiatrist.*** *This novel and the author do not condone what any character may or may not have done, but simply expose how these fictional characters might handle these fictional situations. Fictional characters are not held to the actual letter of the law because they are not actual persons.*

FOUND

ABOUT THE AUTHOR

Found is Julia Biagi's first novel.

Made in the USA
Charleston, SC
29 March 2015